The Great Upending

Also by Beth Kephart

Wild Blues

The
Great
Upending

BETH KEPHART

A Caitlyn Dlouhy Book

ATHENEUM BOOKS FOR YOUNG READERS

New York London Toronto Sydney New Delhi

ATHENEUM BOOKS FOR YOUNG READERS
An imprint of Simon & Schuster Children's Publishing Division

For information about special discounts for bulk purchases, please contact Simon & Schuster Special Sales at 1-866-506-1949 or business@simonandschuster.com.
The Simon & Schuster Speakers Bureau can bring authors to your live event. For more information or to book an event, contact the Simon & Schuster Speakers Bureau at 1-866-248-3049 or visit our website at www.simonspeakers.com.
Also available in an Atheneum Books for Young Readers hardcover edition
Interior design by Debra Sfetsios-Conover
The text for this book was set in ITC Veljovic Std.
Manufactured in the United States of America
First Atheneum Books for Young Readers paperback edition March 2021
10 9 8 7 6 5 4 3 2 1
The Library of Congress has cataloged the hardcover edition as follows:
Names: Kephart, Beth, author.
Title: The great upending / Beth Kephart.
Description: First edition. | New York : Atheneum Books for Young Readers, [2020] | "A Caitlyn Dlouhy Book." | Summary: If eleven-year-old Sara and her brother Hawk can complete a task involving the reclusive author renting out the silo on their farm for the summer, they will receive reward money that will pay for Sara's life-saving surgery.
Identifiers: LCCN 2019004489 | ISBN 9781481491563 (hardcover) | ISBN 9781481491570 (pbk) | ISBN 9781481491587 (eBook)
Subjects: | CYAC: Brothers and sisters—Fiction. | Authors—Fiction. | Marfan syndrome—Fiction. | Heart—Diseases—Fiction. | Family life—Fiction. | Farm life—Fiction.
Classification: LCC PZ7.K438 Gr 2020 | DDC [Fic]—dc23
LC record available at https://lccn.loc.gov/2019004489

For Becca Weust

Full of Shine

Moon's in bloom," Hawk says. "Just hanging there. No strings."

"Big and fat?" I ask. Through the wall that divides us.

"Biggest. Fattest. I'm heading out."

I hear the springs of Hawk's mattress creak. I hear him creep across the floor. I hear the screen in his window go up and his one foot crump and his other foot crump down onto the roof that we call our pier.

"Show's on," he says.

I push up to my elbows. See Hawk through my window, his pale face and his big eyes. He presses his face up against the screen, and then he turns and puts his arms out for balance. The moon pours its bucket of yellow down.

"Coming?" he says, his voice on the edge, in the dark.

I creak up. Put my feet on the floor. Crouch so my hair won't snag on the low rafters, so my head won't scrape. I cross the planked floor and push the screen up and away from the sill. Catch my breath. Swing my daddy long legs and my daddy long arms out into the night, sit down, butt-scoot forward, reach the edge, and throw my legs out into the air beside Hawk's.

Catch more breath.

Fix my vision.

Hawk kicks his bare feet. I kick mine. The air freckles up with fireflies. The trees wave their hands in the breeze. The baled hay we haven't barned up yet looks like waves rushing in.

"Lighthouse is full of shine," Hawk says.

I look where he's looking—toward the old silo where The Mister lives. It's round and it's tall and it's silver. It's got a red front door and a band of windows around its top that blinks on and off.

"You think he's in there?" I ask Hawk, feeling my heart flop around between the bones in my chest.

"Where else would he be?" Hawk whispers, as if The Mister could hear us from all the way here, where we are, which he can't.

"Mom says—"

"I know—" Hawk pulls a stick of dried hay from his hair. He bends it between his fingers. "Shhhh," he says, for no good reason, because I'm already shhhh-ing.

The farm noises up. There are cows in the cow barn, goats in the goat barn, cats in their cuddle, and the old horse Moe, who snorts like a warthog. Also there's Mom and Dad in the kitchen with their decaf, talking low, thinking we can't hear them. Thinking that I haven't heard the latest news, but I've heard it, I've heard it plenty.

Sky is zero clouds and star stuff. It's August 3 and has not rained for twenty-two days. Morning, noon, night, Dad drives his old Ford to the top of the forest hill to check the water in the cistern. The water that feeds the pipes in the house, the cows in the field, the pigs in the sunflower stalks, the goats and their milk, the seeds in the earth. The water that vanishes inch by inch. When it rains, we pull the pots and pans and buckets to the roof and watch the water in them rise. When it rains, Mom hangs the laundry on the old rope to wash. When it rains, Dad checks the cistern so many times Mom sometimes makes him walk so he'll save the gas in the truck.

But now we're on water rations, and here is Hawk and here is me, sitting at the edge of the pier, waiting for our ship to come in.

"Interesting," Hawk says.

He gets to his feet, sets himself up into a crouching rock, and watches. I think about Dad and Hawk and sometimes me, with my helpful height, building those three rooms into that old silo, a Dad scheme to save the farm—another Dad scheme; he's had lots. Each round room sits ten feet above the next round room. A spiral staircase dials through the cutout middle of each floor. Sun pours through the top window band and down the spiral steps and ends in a pretty yellow pool on the first floor. The table and the benches and the bed were built round to fit the round. The last time I was there, the place still smelled like sawdust. It smelled like the refrigerator motor, too, and the lavender wreath Mom had hung.

It was Mom who advertised the place. Mom who wrote the words, and they worked: *Come. Stay.* Sixteen days ago, The Mister drove up the dusty back road in a Cadillac limo so wide and long Hawk gave it a name, and that name is Silver Whale. I'd been down in the garden with my basket and Hawk had been out with the pigs in the stalks and Dad had been up on the hill with the Ford. I'd heard the puttering car, didn't think much of it.

I didn't stand up until I heard Hawk running.

"To the pier!" he said, flying past.

By the time I got in the house and up the stairs and out of my window and onto the pier beside Hawk, The

Mister had arrived. He wore a blue coat, Hawk said, narrating, on account of my eyes. He carted his things from the trunk of the limo through the red of the door by way of the rusty wheelbarrow Dad had left there once the work on the lighthouse was done. He opened the door with the key Mom had left hanging the night before from a little outdoor hook. He was a small man with a hunched back, Hawk said, or maybe he was just hunching under the weight of things. "How many things?" I asked. "Lots," Hawk said.

Come.

Stay.

That was two weeks and two days ago—and all we've figured out since is that The Mister came from far away. He wants his privacy, Mom says. No fresh tomatoes, no slice of pie, no two kids named Hawk and Sara showing up at his front door.

"No prying eyes," Mom said. "Okay? Nobody spying on The Mister."

"Can't help what I see," Hawk said. Mom shook her head.

Now, past the bales of hay that Dad cut and raked and bound, the bales he hasn't loaded yet into the old hay shed, I squint. All I can see through the windows of the lighthouse is a white streak, like a cloud tied to a string.

"Can't figure this," Hawk says, rocking and rocking.

"Can't figure what?"

Hawk rocks. Keeps his figuring to himself, which drives me just about nuts. "Whoa," he finally whispers. "Like a circus act. The guy's wheeling around on a unicycle! Rounder and faster by the minute."

"Unicycle?"

"Serious."

"The old man?"

"Give me a sec."

I wait. Across the dark, under the stars, all I see is that puff of cloud being yanked around by a string. The Mister's hair, it's got to be.

"You rock any harder, you'll fall," I say, because Hawk has stopped reporting again and sometimes it's just too lousy to get your news secondhand, to not see what you want to see, to be relying on your best friend who is your brother. Sometimes I just can't stand that what I see best is my own imagination and not what's out there, in front of me. So that right now I'm seeing with my mind's eye, and what I'm seeing is a figment of thought, by which I mean I half see, half imagine Hawk spying so hard that he tips and he falls into the crunch of apple trees. I half see and half imagine me scrambling through the window and down the stairs and running and Dad calling after me and Mom crying and two kids out of two kids in the Scholl family needing doctors the Scholls can't afford. That's what I see, while Hawk gets to see the actual unicycling Mister.

I catch Hawk's arm in the hook of my own. I yank him back. He falls flat on the roof and looks up and I lie back and something blinks.

"He knows we're here," Hawk whispers, even quieter now. "The Mister."

"You got proof?" I say, my heart flopping hard.

"He turned off the light. Just this second, now. It was on and now it's off and that means that he's seen us."

"Seen you, maybe. Not seen me."

"Like you're not here?" Hawk says. "Like you wouldn't be the easiest of us to see?"

"Stop it," I whisper, louder than him. "Just—"

"Mom can't know, right?" Hawk says. "Mom can't know, and we're not telling."

"You don't tell, I won't tell," I say, and breathe. More trouble is the last thing we Scholls need.

Yellow Orange Red

L iving in the lap of luxury," Dad says.

It's morning, and he's got flapjacks on. They bubble in the skillet. They crisp. He stacks three to a plate and slabs a square of butter up top. Sets out honey from Mom's bees and berries from the berry season, gets our freshly squeezed OJ, gives Mom a kiss. He pulls his black cap down over his red-brown curls and wipes his hands on his jeans, and now we sit like we've got everything we need.

Couldn't raise enough cows, milk enough goats, honey enough bees, thresh enough seeds, crust enough pies to pay for all we Scholls need.

Outside, above the rotten smoosh of the plunked-down apples too small and bitter to eat, the blackflies sing.

"Good ones," Mom says, in compliment of Dad's flapjacks.

"Best of the season," Dad says. Digs in.

Hawk looks at me.

I don't look at Hawk.

We've got our secrets to keep.

We eat.

We eat.

We eat.

"Hear that?" Mom says now.

Dad swipes his cap off, tilts his head. "That Old Moe?" he says.

"Old Moe," Mom says, pulling her hair from her neck on account of the heat. "And the goats."

I put my fork down, swallow hard, listen. That's not just Old Moe. That's not just goats.

"That's the breeders," Hawk says. "The chickens, crying."

"Bear come down from the woods," Mom says. "Must be."

"Couldn't be," Dad says. Mom always thinks of bear first, because bear's her biggest worry. Dad always says whatever he can say so that Mom won't worry. It only works sometimes.

"Snake?" That's Hawk. He hates the squirmy things.

Mom stands, her face full of worry. Dad stands too, and now they crowd in at the kitchen sink and lean toward the window and another of those breeders screams. We hurry to our feet, and because I'm so tall, I see. Over Mom and Dad and through my glasses and through the window: smoke like wisp clouds floating across the roof, too close. Smoke getting grayer. Smoke puffing from behind the house, around the corner, and my heart starts to pound and pound.

"Sara," Mom says now, her voice too calm, scary calm. "Dial 911."

"Mom?"

"Just like we've practiced, Sara. Hawk, you know your part."

We see the smoke. We smell the smoke. We don't see the flames. We stand like we're glued to the floor, too scared to be anything but stuck, and then we're running—through the kitchen and out the back door. Dad to the pond and Hawk to Old Moe and Mom to the shed where we keep our ten-pound ABC extinguisher, the dry-chemical kind, best there is, Dad always says, like buying the right ABC is our best chance of surviving. Maybe it is. I rush for the phone, and the 911 lady picks up and I talk like Mom would want me to. I ask for help, precise and calm. I tell them Scholl farm twice, precise and calm, loud and clear. Saying twice might save us.

"On their way," the lady says, but I know where the engines live, ten miles down the road. I know we're all volunteer out here, and between everything there are miles and hills and the time it takes for people to go running, to go driving, to hop the engine and drive more hills. I know we're in high summer in drought season and the pond is low. I know we can't afford this, but *this* is happening.

The air so heavy when I open the door, and Hawk running Old Moe out of the shed, and the peacocks sloppy and squalling, and Dad calling to Mom and me calling to them—brigade is coming—but now I see where the flames are jumping from, I see where the fire got its start: in the shed where we keep the other half of our hay, which can mean only this one thing: mold heat, spontaneous combustion. Never bale hay too moist, the farm rule goes. Moist makes mold and mold makes heat and heat makes fire in drought season in a barn where everything is dry already, and the hay is half the hay we're counting on to feed all the hay eaters we've got. A jump of fire tries to touch the sun. Another jump, another—through the roof and out the one square window, which isn't white anymore, which is the colors yellow, orange, red, and the fire crackles, it burns, and we'd never bale the hay too soon, but we baled it too soon, must have.

The hay shed is beside the goat shack. The goat shack is beside the breeder birds. The breeder birds are beside the tractor shed. The tractor shed is beside the forest. The house is right here, on the other side of a thin dirt drive—the house with our lives in it, the cellar with my seeds in it, the garage with the machines Dad isn't finished paying for.

Please please please, and the fire burns.

"The goats," Mom calls, working the extinguisher.

"The birds," she calls, and now Hawk is back from parking Old Moe down the long drive, by the Pig Village. He's setting more birds free and running after them, chasing them out of the smoke, and Mom keeps working the extinguisher and her tears burn down her face.

Dad is back and forth, pond to flames, two sloshing buckets in each hand. He's out of breath, but he keeps on running, and the fire is about a thousand licks of flame; it burns brighter and higher with every minute gone. I turn and look down the road for the volunteer brigade, but they're not here yet, and if the siren's screaming, I can't hear it over the sounds of the birds and the goats and the flames. We need the proper hose, the tank of water, the volunteers and their ladders and flameproof boots, and the goats need me, and I turn and run.

"Faster we go, easier we make this," I say, trying to keep my voice steady, trying to persuade Molly, Polly,

Jolly, and Jo out of the dark corner of their own shed, where they're stuck together in a pack—all of them bleating and butting and kicking the hay at their own hooves, feeling the doubled-up heat of the smoke.

"For your own good," I tell those goats. "Come here." If they hear the fear in me, there'll be fear in them. I try for steady, I try for in command. I've got ropes and they've got collars, and I fit them on and tug. It shouldn't be this hard. It is.

"Sara!" Mom calls. "Be careful in there! Be quick!"

I'm careful. I'm as careful as the goats will let me be careful. I'm talking to them, stroking their egos, promising a pig visit—a little grazing between trees. But smoke is in the air that I breathe, and so it's the air they breathe and they resist.

"Come on!" I tug all four at once. "Just! Please!" But they won't budge, and I hear the second-story timbers of the big shed fall, and now maybe parts of the roof, and I hear Dad calling Mom to step away. "You can't save it, love, save yourself."

"I need some help!" I hear Hawk now, chasing the birds. "I need—somebody. Help." I need help too because Molly, Polly, Jolly, and Jo are full of screams.

The smell is hurt in the nose, burn in the eyes. The sound is Dad calling Mom and Mom calling Hawk and the birds screaming. The engines are still down the road—five miles now? three?—and Dad is calling that the pond is too low and that there's not much more water he can dig out with his buckets, and Mom is saying that the ten-pound is empty, gone, no more chemicals, and finally Molly starts to listen to me, stops kicking the floor and tugging away from her rope. She trots in my direction, her deciding done, her better sense succeeding past her scaredness.

"You good girl," I say, hugging her hard, and now, like Molly's the president of the Scholl goats, the others start trotting too, following her lead. I'm out of the goat shed and onto the dusty dirt road, past the ugly black half of the white hay shed, which has no roof now, no window, no second floor, no hay, and I can't stop to look for what is left because if I do, I won't be able to run again. I make it all the way to Pig Village, where Old Moe is tied up to a tree. I loop the goats onto the hooks on the pig shed, check the knots. I tell them, "Listen to Old Moe and the pigs."

"I'll be back," I promise. Turn. Press my hand to my heart and see, down the drive, the flames above the half of the shed that is barely standing there. The hay in the shed is gone and soon the shed will be gone and the fire could keep jumping from dry thing to dry thing, it could take every Scholl thing except the Scholls, and now the earth is trembling beneath my feet, like an earthquake. I turn in the other direction, toward Mountain Dale Road, and even if most of what I see is blur, I know what's coming. I start running, even if I'm not supposed to run, even if I can feel the stretch and pull of the beating heart of me, because it's Charlotte and Jane with their twin pink tractors, coming. It's Mac King with his red slurry tanker. It's Ruth and Michael in their dusty pickup. It's Isaiah in his horse-drawn carriage. The pigs turn like a salute. Old Moe and Molly and Polly and Jolly and Jo hoof at the dirt. I wave my long, long arms, shouting. "Started at the hay shed! We're running out of juice!"

They can't hear me, and it doesn't matter because they know what to do, they have smelled the smoke, they have seen it rise, they have called to each other: Go. The earth quakes harder as they tractor past, truck past, gallop past, get farther down the drive toward Mom, who is running now, toward Dad, who throws the buckets down, and Hawk, who knows how to work a slurry, how to get the water spitting out. Charlotte and Jane have brought their own ABCs. Isaiah's got one too. Ruth and Michael have water tanks in the back of their truck, and now, at last, the yellow truck with its pumps and water is coming.

"Sara," Mom says when I get back down the road. "Take over on the birds." Charlotte throws her wide arm across Mom's thin back. Isaiah is helping with the slurry. It's my job to catch the birds that Hawk set free to save.

We need those birds.

We need everything.

Catch a Bird

Catch a bird, catch a beating heart.

Catch a bird, catch another day's eggs.

Catch a bird, catch a friend, catch a squawk.

Catch a bird, and the fire burns, but it burns less now. The air is singed. When I look back, over my shoulder, from the hill where I've gone, into the trees, where the breeder birds part ran part flew part blew, I see the fire going out and the Scholl farm saved and the brigade and the neighbors and the things they brought because no farm can ever be a lonesome thing. I see Mom and Dad and Hawk inside a circle hug. I see what it looks like when I'm not there, what it might look like, someday. If.

When?

I try not to think that thought.

I think it anyway.

After

Black smoke.
Black char.
Black clouds.
Black earth.
Black hay sticks.

Black leftovers where the hay shed was, like the tooth we pulled from Old Moe's mouth when he couldn't even whinny for the pain.

We're not supposed to cry out here.

We're not supposed to feel what I am feeling.

We're not supposed to be afraid.

Phooey

Pile of lasagna. Three jars of applesauce. Charlotte's preserves and Jane's sourdough—their marriage made in heaven, like they always say, which they pink tractored straight to us, after the fire was bickered back and the goats and Old Moe and the machines were saved and the volunteer brigade did a last pick-through of the hay shed that is no hay shed anymore. We lost some breeders, one of them Hawk's best bird. Hawk's big eyes are full of hurt, his skin is smudge, he's got Band-Aids on his finger burns, and Dad can't stand, and Mom won't sit. Mom just keeps on pacing.

"Lucky, all in all," she says.

And doesn't mean it.

We've lost all the hay that wasn't in the field and all of the hay shed. Every white wall on every other shack or shed is a charcoal mess and the house is yick, it's top to bottom with the smell of burn. No money for scrub. No money for a new shed. No money for the hay we'll need. Insurance takes months. We'll smell like fire for a long time now and the pond is practically gone. New cash problems on top of old cash problems.

We baled the hay when it was damp.

Lucky, all in all.

Charlotte and Jane didn't knock. Nobody does. They just came in, an hour ago, fresh overalls on. They had two baskets in their hands and there they stood, congratulating Mom and Dad on the minimized damage, the good working plan. Congratulating Mac on the excellent condition of his slurry truck, him having water in there instead of cow poop. Congratulating Ruth and Michael for the water in their tank, and Isaiah for his ABC and his horse that galloped up the road, then trotted back and kept Old Moe company beneath the shade of the tree. Old Moe and the goats I saved. Old Moe and the goats and the birds and the pigs. Safekeeping.

"Lucky," Mom said. Her voice flat. Her eyes dark. Her mood black, though she was trying hard to see the luck in our bad luck.

"Bread and jam," Charlotte said. She drummed her chubby fingers over her thin waist. "Straight from our kitchen. Fresh." She has white hair and a young face. Jane stands crooked because of an accident in a ditch and her hair is two long braided ropes, each braid a different rainbow color, and each braid never the same.

"You're—" Mom started.

"You'd do it for us," Charlotte said, scratching the mole near her ear. She's a lady full of twitch.

"Already have," Jane said, "plenty of times and you'd never even count it." She took Charlotte's hand, maybe to stop the twitch, maybe because she could see how hard it was for Mom, standing there talking in the blackness of her mood, to get the two of them back up onto their tractors and home, because the sun was going down and we could already hear Isaiah and his horse on the long drive, heading near with his mother's cheese and his father's jars of sauce, and, after him, Mac, with his lasagna.

"Mildred special," Mac said, when he walked in, and we knew what he meant—that Mildred hadn't fought our fire with her fire because Mildred is always afraid, has always been afraid, since she lost her baby kittens to a fox. Mildred never leaves the house when any danger strikes. Mildred says that she helps best through meat-and-pepper lasagna, and everyone tells Mac to thank her.

"Thank her for us, Mac," Mom said.

"Try to eat," Dad says now, to Mom.

He finds a spatula and cuts us squares. We sit, even Mom sits, and eat off the flapjack plates that Hawk washed a minute ago. We eat lasagna with a side of cheese and another side of sauce. We save the sourdough for breakfast.

"We'll be fine," Dad says, trying to help Mom, and what he means is, *Tomorrow we get up and turn life back on again*, which is one of his sayings, because it was one of those sayings that hang on the wall behind dusty glass to remind Dad, which is to remind us, what our family is made of. Dad's parents died before we were born. This farm became his when he was young. He doesn't talk about the hardest days. He just reminds us of what we're made of.

We eat.

I look at Mom, then look away. She's working on her mood. She doesn't need an audience.

"You hear something?" Mom says, and we all stop the half-heartedness of our chewing and fork scraping so that we can listen. Mom has the best pair of ears in the house. I have the second-best pair.

"Someone at the door," I second her suspicion. "Knocking."

"Strange," Dad says, but there it is again, three soft taps, like someone who doesn't know us, but everybody knows us. Mom gets up. She opens the front door. We leave the lasagna and cheese and follow, all of us smelling like fire and Mildred's lasagna, which is garlic beginning to end.

"Phooey!" Hawk says, when he sees who has come. "Phooey! You're here!" His favorite bird, the smartest one, the best egg layer on the farm, the worst loss of the day, as far as Hawk had been concerned. Phooey is our prize Ameraucana. Lays her sweet green eggs in the cab of Dad's pickup. Has more to say to the pea-hens and the guinea fowls than she does to her own kind, and now she's here—inside The Mister's arms.

Because it's The Mister standing at the door.

His eyes are big and green and bright, and his cotton vest is red, and his shoes are red, but his hands, his face, his hair, his shirt, his pants are snow snow snow. He is a man built out of snow.

He is at our door and Phooey clucks.

"You bad bird," Hawk says, and takes her gently, and doesn't look at me because if he looks at me, The Mister will see how we are looking at each other with the secret we can't tell. Maybe even Mom will see, and Mom's mood can't have cause to get blacker.

"Hard day," The Mister says, "for the farm. I'm sorry." Like he watched the whole thing from his light-house, on his unicycle, circling around. Like he didn't come to help, but he's sorry. He looks sad and tired now, and I know what Mom is thinking. I know that Mom is worried that he'll leave us now, that we'll lose that rent, that we'll go under even more, and that can't happen.

"Yes," Mom says, putting her best face on. "Very hard. Under control now, but hard. Unusual circumstances. We hope . . . Get us some rain and the smell will die down. Get us some rain and—"

"Just came to say I'm sorry, ma'am. And to bring you the bird. Quite a bird. Phooey, you say."

"Phooey," Hawk says.

"Best name I've ever heard for a bird."

Hawk goes red in the cheeks. Looks at me quick. I look away. I look back and now we're all just standing, staring—us at him and him at us. His hair is like a snowdrift. His fingers are longer than fingers should be. His red shoes are very red, the red shining through the dust of the field he must have walked through, from his lighthouse to us, with Phooey in his arms. I notice speckles on his shoes now. I notice speckles on his vest. He sees me staring. Catches my eye and I see and don't have to imagine precisely what Hawk said, last night, seems like a year ago: The Mister saw us spying. The Mister spied on us. Mom can't know. Ever. Secret made and secret kept.

"Grateful," Dad tells The Mister, "for the bird. Real grateful. What do you say, Hawk?"

"Thank you."

"Sara?"

"Thank you, sir." The Mister nods a little. There's a feather on his vest. It shimmers in the falling sun. He sees it. Takes it. Stuffs his pocket with its silky threads.

"Bird seemed a speck bereaved," The Mister says. "Seemed like it wanted to go home."

"Best news of the day," Mom says. "You finding that bird. You want to come in? Join us? We have lasagna."

The Mister shakes his head. His white cheeks turn red. He looks down at the dust and the speckles on his shoes. "Work to do," he says, and waves one hand. He turns and leaves us standing there—Hawk's chin buried in Phooey feathers, Dad's hand buried in the smoky curls up on his head.

"Let's try to finish dinner," Mom says, and that's what we do. Phooey stays in the crook of Hawk's left arm. Our forks scrape our plates.

We eat.

Nobody here wants seconds.

The Thing About Seeds

Dad says that, long time ago, this house was a barn, a place where horses lived and roosters, too, and goats that scared at nothing. After that it was Cow Central, and after that, generations of Scholls before this generation of Scholls turned the Cow Central into the house where we are living now—each generation making its own fix. Each generation turning, like Dad says, a house into a home.

Home is where the Scholls are.

I lie awake. I listen. I think of Molly taking charge. I think of Charlotte and Jane and Mac and Ruth and Michael and Isaiah, slurries and hoses and buckets, the volunteer brigade with the shining truck and the sound of the fire dying. I think of how the wind didn't blow and that kept us safe and how Old Moe kept the pigs tame and nuzzled Isaiah's quarter horse and how the birds screamed holy terror and Hawk couldn't catch them, and then I couldn't catch them, and how not all the birds came back on their own, especially Phooey, who introduced herself to The Mister. The Mister knows our secret and The Mister did not tell. We've lost half our hay and all our hay barn and we smell like smoke and our farm is smoky gray and tomorrow our life will go on, despite there being hardly any water now. Despite the fire stealing the water from our pond.

Life will go on, Dad says. *Every day has a next day coming.* Words from the sayings Dad quotes.

Next day coming.

Sometimes, maybe, I'm not so sure.

The dark air stirs in empty bowls. When the shadows fall, I can hear them. The pipes croak. I picture Dad with the big folds of skin under his eye. I picture Mom and the dagger lines around her mouth. I picture Hawk in the room beside mine—his flashlight on, his book opened wide, his pages turning, Phooey back in the breeder's shed, safe. Hawk reads stories to make our real-life story seem less full of trouble than it is. Hawk reads *Treasure Island* like *Treasure Island* is our cure.

Maybe believing and bravery are the same thing. Maybe I don't have enough of either one in my blood. Maybe I'm not big enough to be who I want to be, which is a really super-strange thing to say, since I'm so very tall. I'm taller than Hawk and I'm taller than Mom and I'm also taller than Dad, and my feet are flat as flapjacks, and also, I have trouble seeing far, and pretty much too much of the time it feels like someone jumped onto my lungs and heart. They've got a name for this, and that name is Marfan syndrome. Marfan. It all comes down to glue. I'm a body built out of stretch. When the doctors tell me what is wrong with me, they show me pictures of my heart, then pictures of my aorta, then pictures of my aortic root. When other people try to guess why I'm so tall and thin, they can say the meanest things, even when they don't mean to be mean, and I always remember what they say, I always remember how it feels. I remember, for example, this one time, when Mom and I drove all the way to the beach so she could teach me her favorite game of all, which is Skee-Ball, how we drove for hours, then we parked. We walked out on the boardwalk, saw the sea. We ate purple cotton candy and nutty fudge, and then we got in line for Skee-Ball.

"Mom," the little girl behind us said. "Mom. Look!"

"Honey," the mother hushed her.

"No," the little girl said. "Seriously. Look, Mom."

I hated that. I hate remembering it now, lying here, when my tongue tastes pretty much like fire, and my teeth do too. We can't wash our hair. We can't blow away the smoke. I can't get the sad stuff out of my head, and now Hawk sighs. Clicks his flashlight. Closes his book. Downstairs, Mom and Dad shuffle off to bed—Dad in his boots and Mom in her flip-flops— and after a while this whole place gets so still that all I can hear is my heart: the spontaneous mutation in my genes, the problem with my proteins. The aorta in my chest bulges, like a fist. It keeps getting bigger; dilation is the word. One year ago, my aortic root measured 3.5 centimeters. Four months ago it measured 3.9. A bigger number is a not good thing. A bigger number means the tissue is thin and getting thinner, and my aorta could break, and after that, 98 percent chances are, I wouldn't be here to tell my story.

Three days ago, Mom and Dad took me to see Dr. G.

Three days ago, I found out the bigger number is getting bigger.

Three days ago, Mom and Dad and I got the news that I'm officially in the danger zone, and all of this was before the fire.

We'd taken the long drive, the three of us. We'd left Hawk to take care of farm things. Dad had put his Deere cap on and Mom had pulled her hair into a pony, and we'd gone hours past white houses and silver silos and red barns and hex signs and a hundred years of rust in a thousand backyards that looked like mostly blur to me. We'd gone down a highway beside a river and then we'd turned toward the city and then Dad parked in the underground garage, the back end of his pickup truck hanging out like a tongue.

We took an elevator that was built like a freezer to Dr. G.'s floor. We waited in chairs covered by zigzag cloth. They gave me that gown the color of kale, that belt the color of broccoli, and then there were rooms and scans and machines and techs, until finally Dr. G. himself arrived, with his purple tie and his kind eyes and his bad news, you could see the bad news in the kind parts of his eyes. Mom held my hand. Dad swiped the cap off his head. All the way home in the cab of the truck, we didn't say a thing, and when we got home, I said, "Hey, you, Hawk, you like your lonesome day?" because what was I supposed to say?

You're so brave, the doctors say to me, but I'm not brave. I'm just a kid who has some problems with her proteins. I'm just a kid who loves her farm and the people on the farm, the animals and birds and even snakes on the farm, and, for the record, I've never seen a bear. I've got eggplant and tomatoes and lettuce and carrots and zucchini and onions and sweet peas and the start of kale in my garden. I've got a museum of seeds in the cellar. I've got threshers and I've got jars and I've got Mom and Dad and Hawk and us, and do you want to know the best part about seeds, the thing I know that helps me breathe when it gets late like this and I'm full of worry?

Every seed contains the future.

Every seed is like a promise we shouldn't break. Every seed, and I'm lying here, remembering, staring hard into the dark until the near air breaks into grays and blacks and shadows and the shelves with their things are real to me, and I am real to me, I can't help myself, I can't stop myself, my mind is full of whirl, and I'm remembering.

I am four and Hawk is three and we make a neat fit in the front seat of the Ford pickup, between Dad at the wheel and Mom on the other side. We're headed down Mountain Dale for the Bunions' fresh ice cream. It's peach season and the ice cream will be thick with fruit, the fruit hard as ice until I hold it in my mouth and it thaws out and becomes tender sweet. And Mom's singing. And we're driving.

I am five and Hawk is four and Old Moe is having a party. "Ten years old today," Dad says, strapping a party hat to Old Moe's head so that he looks like a unicorn now, but only for a minute, because the horse bucks and off the hat flies. Off Old Moe's head and over the fence. It gets picked up with some breeze and then it falls and Hawk catches the hat with the top of his boot, like a horseshoe pole would ring a horseshoe, and Mom says that Hawk wins and we want to know: Hawk wins what? "Hawk wins the first piece of Old Moe's pie," Mom says, and it's a really good pie, a summer pear pie, and we all have to wait, after dinner that night, until Hawk eats the first slice, which he eats so slow, in honor of Old Moe, he says, slow enough that Mom finally says, "All right, Hawk. That's enough. Now it's everybody's turn."

I am six and Hawk is five, and the yellow bus stops on Mountain Dale Road and lets me off at the end of our farm drive. Mom is waiting for me, and Hawk, too, a big sunflower in his hand to welcome me home, the bright droopy thing in Hawk's hand, almost as tall as him and dropping dried seeds out of itself. "Sweetie, what's wrong?" Mom asks me, because she can see my tears even though I'd tried to rub them off, even though I didn't want her to hear what the other kids were saying. Hear it from me, which she will, if she asks.

"What's wrong?" Mom asks again, and I am not two minutes off the bus or ten steps down our drive when I start telling Mom the whole mess of it, how the kids at school were making fun of how tall I am, making fun of my long feet, making fun of my smile. I'm telling Mom through crying, and Hawk is pulling that sunflower behind, the end of the stalk dragging up dust, and I want to know why I'm different, I want to know *if*

I'm different, and Mom says, "Why don't we see some-one who knows more than we do, and see if he can give us some answers?"

"What do you mean *someone*?" I ask. I remember being that young and that size. I remember standing there, asking.

"I'm thinking we might visit with a doctor," Mom says, which is how I know she's already given thought to it, the doctor part, that she's been worried herself, that she's been hoping for a why, that maybe I look a little bit like I need answers, and maybe Dad and maybe Hawk know it too, but none of them ever men-tioned it, none of them wanted me to worry.

I am six and Hawk is five and I remember, because this is how it all began, and I remember what the doc-tors said, one doctor after another until we found a doctor who knew, who would say the word "Marfan," who would tell us the truth. Marfan is not a disease, it's a disorder. It's not one symptom, it is many. It is not a single path, it is not a predictable future; every person who has Marfan has a different life to live. "Ever hear of Sergei Rachmaninoff?" the doctor said. This was Dr. G., the one and only Dr. G. "The composer and pianist? Some believe that he had Marfan, and look what he did: used the length of his fingers to reach the piano keys that he needed, used the height of his body to conduct the orchestras."

"Never heard of him," I said.

"Abraham Lincoln, then," Dr. G. said. "You've heard of him? Our sixteenth president. Long and very thin, with a narrow, narrow chest? Could have been Marfan. That's what some have said."

I wasn't sure what this had to do with me in those days, back then. Maybe I'm still not sure, but I remember. I remember Mom and Dad and Hawk on the way home, because we could still fit four across back then. I remember sandwiches for dinner, glasses of water, not much that anyone said. I remember Mom telling me the next day that sometimes we don't have a choice about what happens to us, and that what had happened to me was called "spontaneous." That there are plenty of people diagnosed with Marfan, beautiful and smart people, geniuses and leaders, had I been listening to Dr. G.? "This doesn't change who you are, Sara," Mom said. "It just changes some of how you might live." I remember her telling me that. And maybe I wished that having a word for what I had could change who I was, that having a name for this thing would bring a change to this thing, make me shorter than I was, make my teeth do what teeth are supposed to do, which is come in nice and straight, make my feet all arched and graceful.

But that's not how it works at all.

I am seven and Hawk is six, and September to June

we get up early for chores, we have our flapjacks for breakfast, we ride the school bus to school and ride the school bus back from school, Hawk sitting with me or else behind me now, so nobody on that bus can say a thing about how tall I am, am I a secret giantess, why do my fingers bend backward like my fingers do, am I a real person or a witch? They won't say it to me when I am near and they won't say it around the teachers, not anymore, and I feel good anyway, I'm little by little finding the pride in myself, because I get the best grades in my class of twelve, I get the As on my spelling and my numbers and my stories. I get the As on the projects we have, and Hawk is near, beside me, and I don't think about Marfan, mostly, and I don't let it stop me. We're keeping a watch on it. That's what we do. Doctor checkups and doctor check-ins, and then I pretend it isn't true.

There are chores when we get home. There are things to do, and then work for school, and then dinner, and I am eight and Hawk is seven, I am nine and Hawk is eight, I am ten and Hawk is nine, I am eleven, and I have to tell the truth by now: I am getting tired. It sounds weak to me, it sounds all wrong, I'm just a kid, I saved my brother, once, from drowning in the pond, I saved my father, once, from falling off a roof, I saved my mother, once, from an angry cow, I saved my goats, and I saved my seeds, I saved all those seeds,

I saved the future. I am not a natural giver-upper, but I cannot keep up. More and more I am not myself, until one day, I'm alone with Mom and Dad, telling how sometimes it hurts to breathe, how sometimes I cannot catch my breath, how sometimes I just don't want to get up at all. They listen hard. Dad holds one hand. Mom runs her fingers through my hair, and I can feel the hurt in them.

They make an appointment the next day with Dr. G., a different kind of appointment, not a regular checkup. In three days, on a Tuesday. Hawk will be at school. Hawk will go home with a friend. Hawk will be mad because he wants to come too, this isn't fair, this is family business. They drive me back to the hospital that is so far away, and we ride the elevator, and we wait our turn, and they do their tests, and it's her heart, the doctors say, Dr. G. says it. "The aortic valve is leaking," he says. "We'll need to keep a watch." After that, he says something else: "The bend of the bones in her chest is a problem. Layman's terms: her lungs don't have enough room to breathe."

Dr. G. says it to Mom and Dad, and then he says it to me, and he wonders: Do we understand?

Mom nods. Dad doesn't.

What I understand is that something big has changed. That after all the regular checkups and check-ins, the keeping an eye on it, the let me know if something's shifted, something's shifted: the symptoms have gotten worse. That who I thought I am is not who I now am, though Mom keeps saying, in the truck, going home, "You're the same Sara, Sara. Don't forget that." Mom says we are defined by the choices we make and the goodness we are and our grace in the face of beautiful things and not the science of our genes or the quality of our luck or the money in our banks. She says I am an A plus-er, top of the class when it comes to every-thing that counts, and that I'm not to forget that, and we have doctors to trust, and we're going to listen more closely to my body now, we're going to keep a different kind of watch on this. We're going to take care of this, and Sara, I am sorry.

She is so sorry.

I'm still eleven and Hawk is still ten. I'm listening to my body and it hurts to listen, hurts to hear, hurts to breathe, and now, sometimes, I'm taking a week off from school for being so tired, then another week off from school for the same excuse, then a few more days, and I'm falling behind, I'm losing track of home-work and projects and grades, I'm starting to panic. Too much being sick, too much panic. Mom says maybe we should think of other options. I ask her what kind. She says what would I think if I did school from home now, if we learned mostly the same things, but differently.

"More time to rest, Sara," Mom says, telling me how

it would work. "More setting our own schedule. More choices. I think it would be fun, anyhow, could be fun, and I think I'd learn a lot, and I'd like that chance, and I wonder: What do you think, Sara? Do you think home-schooling could help?"

Homeschooling, Mom says, and I can tell she's been giving it a lot of thought, that she's looked into it, close, talked to my teachers, I don't know when. She's been watching me, but still it takes me another week to decide. Another week for me to leave all my As behind, my reputation as the smartest, the kids who had stopped teasing, the kids who maybe would have asked, if Hawk wasn't always close, if they weren't afraid of repercussions, how it feels to be a giantess. I'm not leaving because of any of that. I'm not leaving because of shame. I'm leaving because my heart wants me to. Because here on the farm, in my own time, I'll find new ways to stand up to Marfan.

"I'm not going if she's not going," Hawk says, when he finds out.

"Hawk," Mom says, her voice even and low. We're sitting in the kitchen. Flapjacks done. Dad outside. Figgis, my tuxedo cat, weaving around our legs beneath the table.

He crosses his arms. He's absolute.

"This is about Sara, honey."

"Right."

"Right?"

"If it's about her, it's about me."

"I know you're—"

"We, Mom. We. We're family."

"Hawk."

"Nope."

"We can't just—"

"It isn't fair. You can't give her this and not give it to me."

"We're not giving . . ."

"Yes, you're giving."

He pushes back on his chair. He grabs Figgis by the scruff. He runs up the stairs and he shuts his door and I hear it lock and look at Mom.

"It'd be more fun," I say, "if Hawk homeschooled too."

"Hmmm," Mom says. "Hmmm." She shuts her eyes. She hadn't expected this. Marfan makes my mother tired.

I nod a yes for Hawk, even though she can't see me. I stare hard at her, willing her, hoping. There are shadows underneath her eyes and silks of gray I never saw before falling forward from her bandanna. My mother has a perfect turned-up nose. Her lips are pale and chewed on.

"I'll talk to Dad," she says, after a long, long time. Her eyes are still closed. The kitchen smells of hot syrup. I don't know when she does decide, but it's settled before dinner.

I am eleven, and Hawk is ten, and we are new homeschoolers. We take our lessons at the kitchen table, and in the barn, and on the farm. Lessons from Mom and Dad, from the books that come in the brown envelopes, fat and proud in our mailbox. From the history and math and science and machines of the farm. From the miracle stuff of water, birds, and trees, the clouds we can see, and the stars. When we take our state tests, we always ace them because we are still A plus-ers, we won't let Mom and Dad down, or each other, or the farm, and this is how the days are, this is what I remember, and my mind whirls whirls whirls whirls.

Pie

riday is pie day and today is Friday, and no fire is getting in the way of pie, no news. Mom's already up at the five o'clock hour, starching and sugaring and cinnamoning the berries, rolling the crust, fluting the edges.

I hear the pour and pop, the hot bump the oven makes when it reaches temperature, the scrape of the foil pans against the metal racks, the yap of Mom's flip-flops. Mom was a Jersey Shore girl before she married Dad. There are some things she won't give up. Like the polka-dotted polish on her toes and the noise of her flip-flops and the soft crush of the faded beach hat, which she prefers over a John Deere cap. Dad says he fell in love with Mom as soon as he saw her dancing to a radio song on the Wildwood boardwalk. Mom says it took her a whole lot longer to fall in love with Dad, but then she did. Then we two kids arrived, and she gave her love of the sea to Hawk and me.

Mom learned pie baking from Dad's mother before either Hawk or I were born. She uses the same *Farm Journal* recipes that were passed on to her. "Goodness doesn't need improving," Dad will say, when he rounds the corner and takes a look at Mom's pie-baking commotion.

Now it's closer to dawn and Phooey's quiet, most of the birds are quiet. Verdi the rooster has been quiet since three a.m., when he had his opera moment. It's Mom I still hear rolling the dough, pouring the sugar, keeping her radio on with her oldies music, and now the black in my room has turned a misty blue that will soon enough be pink. The skies are big, are coming. I hear Dad's boots downstairs, rasping the floor, I hear him rounding in toward Mom. The high and the low of their talk.

"Hawk," I whisper to the wall between us. "Hawk?"

But when Hawk's asleep, he sleeps.

If I stay in bed an hour more, all the pies will be in their white boxes with the lids cracked open to ease the heat. If I stay an hour and a half, Dad will be back in from the barns where now he's gone, back from his talk with Old Moe, back from his pickup ride to the cistern, back to making flapjacks. Dad will be back from studying the hay barn, which is not a hay barn anymore. Dad will smell like cinders.

Peach Marshmallow Pie. Cherry-Mincemeat Pie. Oatmeal Pie. Pecan Puff Pie. Farmer's Peanut Pie. I can tell from the smells that Mom's going for broke, with her evaporated creams and egg-white toppings. She's going to extremes like she does when she has to put her sadness somewhere. I get up and put on my jeans. The ones Mom sewed an extra three inches of flowery-paisley bell-bottom hemming to so my ankle bones wouldn't show through my socks. I pull my light T-shirt with the three-quarter sleeves over my head. I comb my fingers through my hair. I turn my bracelet around for luck. It's not a shower day. I use the toilet but don't flush. I brush my teeth quick and splash some water on my cheeks, my chin.

I head to the kitchen.

"Pies are fluffing," Mom says, snapping off the radio, wiping her eyes with the cuff of her shirt, not turning. She says it as if the pies don't always fluff, as if she's not the best pie baker in this whole 872-person town, in any town, probably. Mom wins the pie contest at the county fair every September. The Peach Marshmallow is cooling on the rack, the Oatmeal and Pecan Puff too.

The Farmer's Peanut is still in the oven, and there's an Apricot Chiffon in a white box with a popped lid.

Mom says that it's important that everybody in every life gets to choose the things they love. Mom chose pies, and when she isn't baking pies, she can fix any tractor that Dad breaks.

I could too, if I were strong enough. I could too, if the doctors weren't always telling me to be careful, Sara, be careful, Sara, don't want to strain your heart.

Some things can get fixed.

Some things can't.

I'll tie the boxes shut with a string when all the pies are cool enough. Hawk will drive them the two country miles to Rayuda's Diner, where Sal is already waiting for him—Sal and the early crowd, pies for breakfast, gossip for the trouble. Nobody minds Hawk out on the road in his tractor, out behind the horse-drawns, beside the lumberyard's big wheelers. Hawk's been driving that tractor for two years, probably more, and out here it's not your age that matters. Out here, it's about your skills. You drive the tractor right, they wave at you friendly. They always wave to Hawk. He drives steady so the pies won't slide. He drives up and over to where the diner crowd is waiting. He's just like the rest of us. He does any job he needs to do, and he does it. Scholl-style well.

I step into the kitchen. Mom gives one last pinch to

the crust of her final pie and slides it into her double-wide oven.

"We haven't talked about you," she says. "We need to talk."

"Hay barn burned," I say. "We've got other worries."

"We still need to talk about you," Mom says. "We don't forget one thing because of the other."

She makes a quick rinse of her hands and turns. The shadows underneath her eyes don't move when she moves. The knuckles on her hands are red with ache. The polka-dotted paint on her toes could use a fixing. "We can't keep putting it off, Sara. We have to talk it through."

"Don't feel like talking about it," I say. "Okay?"

"Sara."

"Mom," I say. "It can wait."

"We are not waiting."

"Fire's worse than some root."

"No, Sara. Actually—"

"Fire's just as expensive."

"Actually—"

I hear Hawk on the steps and turn. I see his crease-y Doc Martens with the laces untied, his skinny black jeans, his belt pulled to the last notch, his yellow T-shirt like a caution sign. His eyes are two moons, day or night.

"What were you talking about?" he says.

"Nothing," I say. Mom gives me a look.

"Were so," he says. "Heard you."

"Not everything's your business, Hawk." Mom looks like she could cry. Mom hates more than anything to cry, and I hate, even more than that, when Mom cries and she's crying over me. If you love someone, you shouldn't hurt them. I know I'm hurting Mom. Mom isn't answering Hawk.

"Peach Marshmallow Pie. Cherry-Mincemeat Pie. Oatmeal Pie. Pecan Puff Pie. Farmer's Peanut Pie. Apricot Chiffon," she says, like everything's fine. "One more in the oven, and we're done." Her pretend-fine voice isn't so great at pretending.

Hawk touches the key he wears around his neck, the key to the John Deere he unbuilt and built beside Dad, Mom supervising. It's 9,585 pounds of ding and rust and you'd think it couldn't run, but Hawk makes it do what he needs.

"Twenty minutes till breakfast," Mom says. "An hour till the pies are cool enough for travel."

Hawk stands there. Stuck.

"Sourdough and jam," Mom says. "We'll heat it in the oven. Hawk?"

He shakes his head, stares hard at me. I read his eyes better than anybody living on this planet, and he's the last thing from pleased.

"I'm going outside," he says.

"Okay," I say.

"I'm looking for Dad," he says. "And for Phooey."

"Stay away from the hay barn," Mom says, like the black stub of what's left could burst into flames again. Like he'd go in there to sulk.

"I'm looking for Dad," Hawk says again. "I want to ask him something."

"We can talk, if you want," Mom says. "Later, we can talk."

"Whatever."

The back door opens and then it slams. A cat meows. The breeders squawk.

Ask Me

A sk me if I can help it.
Can't.
Ask me if I'm sorry.
Am.
Ask me how I'm supposed to explain to Hawk that the news is bad. My bad news is his bad news. How am I supposed to say it?
Won't.
Ask me how Mom is still standing here, baking her pies like it's just another Friday, like the hay shed isn't gone and the whole place doesn't smell like smoke, like Dr. G. didn't say what Dr. G. said.

"Hawk?" I call out after him. "Hawk!"

But when I open the back door and see him out near where the hay barn used to be, I see him holding Phooey, crying.

Dad's truck is gone, but it will come back.

"Hawk?"

T in the Road

I hear the John Deere rumbling up the last hill, and now it hits our drive.

I crush a few more dried basil seed heads over the threshing screen, then stop, shake the bowl below, blow the chaff away. In a few days I'll take these seeds and slide them into a plastic sleeve and put them in the freezer to kill the tiny pests that could mess them up. A few days after that, I'll move the sleeves to the darkest shelf in the cellar corner that I call (everybody calls) Sara's Museum of Seeds. Basil seeds are black as pepper. They live inside dried flower heads. You have to wait until they're dry as death before you can rescue them for a new round of living. Basil seeds can live a whole five years of doing zero in the dark and still be ready to come to life again. You just have to crack the earth at the right time.

Crack the earth.

That's how Dad says it.

We don't talk about what the seeds *really* mean. Why they mean so much to me.

At the curve in the drive, I hear Hawk's tractor tires thump. I hear the pigs rushing back to the lookout posts in their red-shack village, the heads of the sunflowers swishing. The dirt drive runs a brown river between trees. Civil War trees, Dad calls them. Dad says the trees were here before he was, and before his father was, and maybe even before his grandfather was, and absolutely before the words that hang in the frames. It's history everywhere at the Scholls.

"Sara," Mom said, "Hawk'll be all right." Because we never had our family breakfast. Because Dad didn't come back, and neither did Hawk. Because Mom had to go talk to Hawk all by herself and help him pack the pies and give him a hug to send him off.

Hawk's not all right. I'm not all right. Who *is* all right? The smell of fire everywhere.

I carry the threshed seeds to the porch and leave them there for later freezing. I walk toward the drive, toward the tornado of dust that Hawk is making. He sees me and throws the skinny of his arm out toward me like he's a human windshield wiper. He drives his tractor into the shed where all the tractors and the trucks live side by rusting side. He could say a million things, ask a hundred questions, make me say I'm sorry, but he hops out, he's running. Running fast, and running past.

"To the pier," he says, and I'm coming.

Spyglassing

He's on the edge of the roof by the time I climb out, his yellow shirt blaring, his feet kicking. He has his binoculars up to his eyes—a country-fair auction special that he prefers to call his Spyglass. He dials in and out, breathes heavy.

"You should wear a sign," I finally tell him. "Hey. Look. Over here. I'm a spy."

"You've got a front-row seat," Hawk says, "on a Spyglass situation."

I lean back on my elbows, feel the early-morning heat inside the roof tar, close my eyes, say a little silent thank-you to my best-friend brother who is talking to me, finally. I hear the cows out there in a morning moo, the ducks on the low, low pond, the loose laces of Hawk's Doc Martens making tiny ticks with every kick, and I wish I could make Hawk laugh. I hear him dialing in and out, perfecting his surveillance. I hear him holding off on questions.

"Sweet Davy Jones," Hawk says, after a while. "She sure is stylish."

I sit up and open my eyes. See the blurry glisten of the lighthouse. A second car sits beside the Silver Whale. A pink blur stands at the lighthouse door. Or maybe it's a pink blur's shadow. Beneath my glasses I rub my eyes. It doesn't help. It never does. I make a grab for Hawk's Spyglass. He swivels away so I can't take it.

"She passed me on the road," Hawk says. "New York plates on a brand-new Rover. Trouble. Had her hand on the horn for half of Mountain Dale. I thought Isaiah's buggy was going to jump the rut."

"You talk to her?" I want to know.

"I talked to her," Hawk says. "She pulled right up beside me, waved at me to cut the engine. 'You know any strangers come to town?' she asked me. I said, 'No, ma'am.' 'You know this man?' she asked me, showing me a photograph. 'Can't say as I do,' I said."

"You said that?" My brother's near beside himself. Telling a story with one single breath.

"'Course I said that. Rules are rules, right? Mom said."

"Right." I'm glad for this, glad for Hawk talking like he isn't mad.

"'You know someone I can speak to?' the lady said," Hawk says. "'Not many people around here,' I told her. 'Not that many to talk to.' She was rolling up her window before I was done. Punching numbers into her phone. Waving me off like *I* was the one who'd stopped her on the road. By the time she passed me again, she was zipping. She took the loop, Sara. The loop. What stranger you ever heard of knows something about our loop?"

The loop being the back way in, the second drive, the road that leads straight to The Mister, which is where she is now, knocking at the lighthouse. "Guess somebody told her something," I say.

"Guess. So why was she asking me?"

"You're looking real sly, Hawk," I say. "One hundred percent incognito." I make another Spyglass grab. My brother's quick. He blocks but doesn't tackle.

"Lady's talking a blue streak," Hawk says, ignoring me like he can. "Only thing is," he continues, "she's talking to the door. The Mister must not be in the mood for company."

"Maybe The Mister's out watering the pigs," I say. "Somebody has to."

Hawk sighs, a real quick sigh. He does a 360-degree Spyglass sweep. "No sign," he reports, "of The Mister.

But also: wait. Yeah. She's carrying something. A box. A big—"

"What kind of box?" I say.

"Wait," Hawk says again. "She's giving up. She's—" He's whispering like the lady could hear him across the whole stretch of the fields. I wait for Hawk's report, for a shift in the action, a twist in the plot, a rev in the Rover, a tornado of dust, and I'm so sick of waiting that I make another grab for the old Spyglass, and Hawk doesn't put up a fight.

"Well, will you look at that," I say.

Hawk whistles, long and low. "You see what I see?" he says, and I do, I see it now, I see the lady with her white-blond hair and her pale pink dress and her spike-heel shoes. I see her white Rover and I see that box, but not a regular box. More like a banged-together box built out of thick planks of wood. The box is so heavy, box is so wide, box is so big, she's weaving right and left on her silly shoes, and now she drops the box and bends in half and drags and nags and pulls, until, at the red door of the lighthouse, she drops the box and stops.

She heavy breathes. Her dress is high on her thighs. She yanks it kneeward.

She pounds the door.

She talks her streak.

She tugs her dress, throws up her arms, and turns,

wobbling back to the Rover. All this way, she's come. And The Mister isn't answering.

She opens the door to the Rover. Slides in. Stays put. Finally engines up.

"Lady's in full retreat," I report to Hawk.

He has heard the Rover roar.

He has seen the sheets of dust.

He has seen The Mister, like now I see The Mister, in the third-floor window of the lighthouse. Standing up there. Both hands on his hips. His forehead on the glass. Looking down.

"A man in hiding," Hawk says, his eyes big.

"What from?"

"A woman and a box."

"What do you make of it?"

"Mystery," Hawk says. "Pure and simple."

No mystery is pure and simple.

"Sara?" we hear Mom now. "Hawk?"

He's off the roof in half a second.

He'll cut Mom off at the pass.

Phooey, Again

"Phooey's done it again," Mom says. Says it to Hawk, out in the back, near the scorch, where Hawk has gone to give me time to crawl back into the house unheard—roof through window, down the stairs.

I sneak back out to where I'm supposed to be—out in the side garden with my pink basket, checking the full-sun crops in the beds I built, the eggplant and the peppers and the squash. Out by the char they talk, near the breeder birds, and I slip on past, Hawk giving me cover.

"That Phooey," Mom repeats herself now. "That ridiculous bird."

That beautiful bird, she means, with her muff and her beads and her red streak and her extra-sensitive tail. Phooey lays eggs with a touch of green, every egg a version of Easter. Phooey can walk among the peacocks and still be the primo bird, can leave her feathers wherever she wants without a scolding. Phooey came home in the arms of a stranger, and now she is missing again. Every hour, another trouble. She knows where she's supposed to be, and she always goes free-ranging somewhere else.

I hear Hawk calling out for Phooey, headed up toward the woods, and Mom cutting down to the shed where just last week the youngest goats had had their clove-oil cure. No horns make for better goats, Mom says, and she's the only one among us we trust to get the injections right—keeping the needle flat against the goats' skulls when she injects the stuff into their horn buds. She doesn't hurt them. She helps them, she says. It helps me, sure enough, to milk goats that don't have horns.

I pull the weeds from between the greens, check the chipmunk fence, pinch free whatever's ripe to eat or sell, listen to Hawk calling out for his bird. I walk my basket across the garden and into the house and set it down by the silver kitchen sink and go back outside where the peacocks scoot. Maybe Phooey went off to the pigs. I start on down the road.

The cows are far, the soybeans near. The evergreens look like giants in green skirts on either side of the road. It's a long walk to Pig Village when you walk it slow. I walk it slow.

We've got twenty-six pigs in the Village and a bunch of stiff sunflowers. Twenty-six pigs the color of ivory soap, the color of ash, the color of pie crust, some of them spotted. The pigs see me coming and they start running and all I can see for a time is the swish of the sunflowers over their heads.

There's not a drop of rain in the sky.

The pigs follow me back to their shacks, where their water buckets sit inside old tires.

"Move it," I tell the pigs. "Come on." Nudging Mr. Dance this way and Mr. Livesey that, until we reach the spigot and the hose. I turn the water on, fill each bucket, snap the water off, quick. Stand where I am to catch my breath. Sit down, because I'm dizzy.

"Mind your own business," I tell the pigs. And then I tell them what they already know. They're noisy and they're gross and I lots of love them, even if they do belong to Hawk, even if he's named a bunch of them for the characters in his *Treasure Island.*

Out on the road, Isaiah's horse is clopping and now a big truck from the lumberyard speeds through and then Johnny Gold's '55 Mustang, which he drives because he likes the show of it. Looking for water, I think. Looking for rain. Looking for trouble in August.

We've got plenty of trouble, I could tell him. Want some of ours? It's free.

There's a white blotch of sun in the east sky. There's a black scorch where the hay barn was. There's cut hay in the field that we'll have to loosen up so it can dry. No more mold. No more combustion. Nothing spontaneous.

She'll need to take care, Dr. G. said. *We'll need to watch her.*

I watch Hawk's pigs slurping the bottoms of their buckets, sponging the metal with their collapsible snouts. Hawk'll come later with the tomato seeds and onion skins, the back ends of the watermelons, the leftover corn and soy, the stuff he wheels in the wheelbarrow. Hawk will come, after he finds Phooey.

I stand and back away from the pigs, toward the road. The sunflowers swish and their petals singe, and in a couple of weeks it will be harvesttime, the seed coats black and white and plump in the heads. I'll bang the seeds loose. I'll dry them super dry. I'll store some in the cellar, and sell some at the market, and bake some for eating and split the hulls with my tongue, if there is time for all that. If.

The story of a seed is the story of tomorrow.

When I reach the part of the road that cuts beside

the hayfields, I feel something that wasn't there before, and turn.

I see—can't really see.

I think—something.

A shadow, maybe.

A shuffle?

"Hello?" I say. But no one answers. Nothing moves. Slower now, I walk the road. Behind me again I hear the crunch of stone, the rub of something on the road.

This time when I turn, I see a thin and disappearing shadow.

"Hello?" I say.

Nothing.

"Hello?" I say it again.

The pigs don't come this far. The cows are behind their fences. Old Moe doesn't leave his barn unless he's bridled up and ready, and if it were Hawk or Mom or Dad or any other farmer, they'd have said hello by now.

It has to be The Mister.

I cross my arms.

Not one thing happens.

There is pig talk in the distance, birds.

"Hello?" I say.

And nothing.

I need Hawk out here. I need my brother. I need someone to answer.

If I Could

I would:
   Tell Hawk everything.
I would:
Tell him not to worry.
I would:
Ask him to help me not to worry.

Red Flannel Hash

Mom's in the kitchen by the time I get back to the house. She's making Red Flannel Hash. She needs onions and potato help. She puts the corned beef to rest, and then the beets. She takes the sour cream from the refrigerator. Dad came in with hay in his cap and the smell of cow all over, and Mom said he'd have to scrub up outside, which is what she does when she wants to talk, just the two of us.

We're side by side, listening to radio songs, trying not to smell the stink of the fire, but the stink's still here. The stink is living in my nose. We're side by side with our spoons and knives. Mom talks. I have to listen.

"Your father and I will find a way, Sara. You have to have the operation."

"Can't afford it," I say.

"Can't afford to lose *you*," she says.

"Why can't we just—"

"Sara."

She uses her best calm tone, her best calm words. Her hair falls out of her bandanna and into her face. She says what she has wanted to say, that Dr. G. had had another consult with his colleagues and that when I was out watering the pigs, Dr. G. called.

"Dr. G. has been talking to his colleagues, Sara," she says. "They are working out the plan."

"Don't want to hear about it."

"It's called the David procedure, Sara. It'll spare your valve. If it works out right—and it will work out right—you'll be good as new. Less risk of a stroke. Less risk of endocarditis, which is a kind of inflammation. No blood thinners needed. No machine in your heart after that. Best operation there is."

"No operation is a good operation." I slam the knife down, quartering potatoes. I slam it again, halving the quarters.

"Best surgeons for the David are in Cleveland," Mom says, doing nothing but talking now, doing nothing but looking at me, and now at the knife in my hand, which she takes away, pushes off the cutting board.

"Ohio?"

"Dr. G. is talking to Cleveland," Mom says. "Dad is talking to the banks."

"Since when have the banks ever helped us?"

"Sara. We have to—"

We hear Hawk's boots on the porch, boots in the kitchen. Mom's got my knife in her hand, and I can barely see through the way I feel, and Hawk's got Phooey in his arms, and I hear them, two eggs in his pockets.

"Fugitive arrest!" Hawk says, and he might have wanted to laugh, but he's not. He's looking at Mom and looking at me and I have no idea how much he's heard.

"Time to put that bird on curfew," Mom says, but she doesn't mean it. She just wants to save Hawk from the talk she's had with me. She just wants us easy, family. She hooks one arm over Hawk's shoulders and the other over mine and pulls us all so close that that bird drops some feathers to the floor. I feel Mom's heart, and it's hurting, and now Hawk tells us all about it—how he found Phooey up on the hill, in the spiderweb cabin someone built before we lived here and no one has lived in since. There's nothing but stained mattresses and a rusty sink in there, a couple of plastic buckets in there. Somebody, or maybe a storm or maybe a bear, whacked out the window long ago, so the wind blows in, the loose seeds and leaves, the snow in winter, the squirrels and chipmunks and mice, the bees that don't make honey, and Phooey, Hawk is saying, who must have squawked up that hill and hopped inside and settled down in the fluff of the split mattress.

"I talked to her the whole way down the hill," Hawk finishes his story. "I talked to her and she didn't talk back. Bird knows she's in trouble."

He strokes her head the entire time he's talking.

That bird will never be in trouble.

Mom unhugs us. Hawk looks up, and it's almost like he looks up and then looks through me. We get the dinner on. Dad comes back, and Mom and I can't talk anymore about the operation I need but will never have.

"You set the table, Hawk," Mom says, and he does.

"You get the vase out, Sara."

"Ma'am."

Dad goes outside to the wildflower patch and brings some fresh-cuts in.

"Nice," Mom says when he's done, because Dad's a real good flower arranger, and because now it's time to eat together, to appreciate all we have.

Shuffle in the Shadows

I don't tell Hawk about the shuffle in the shadows until the white balloon of the sun pops and the sky breaks into its berry colors and the night comes in with all its stars, and Hawk and I are alone again, the Spyglass pressed to his eyes, and I don't even try to grab it. I don't want him to get mad, or madder. I don't want him to ask what Mom was saying about Dr. G. and Cleveland, and I don't want him to look at me like I'm keeping secrets from him.

"Box is gone," he reports, his voice flat.

"The special delivery?"

"Looks like. Someone has dragged it straight out

of sight. Or maybe dragged it inside." Hawk shrugs, casual, like he's not itching to know.

"What's it mean?"

"Have no idea. An interesting development."

Hawk keeps his eyes pressed to his Spyglass. He watches the light of the lighthouse, which even I can see is third-floor bright. Nothing happens, and we're just waiting, and he's not talking, even though he's the talker, so I tell Hawk about watering his ornery pigs. I tell him how I cut back through the sunflower patch and got to the road between the trees and how I started hearing things. The sound of a shuffle, I say. The sound boots make when their person won't pick up their feet.

"Not an animal on this farm that does the shuffle," Hawk says, his voice getting some life back up into it. "Unless it was those geese."

"It wasn't geese. It wasn't anything but boots. Swear on it."

"But you didn't see it." Hawk lowers his Spyglass.

"Shadows is all I saw."

"Curiouser and curiouser," Hawk says. He kicks his legs into the dark. Lifts his Spyglass. "Only one person it could be on that road at that hour," he says at last. "Gotta be The Mister."

"Of course," I say. "But still. No reason for The Mister to be following me."

"No reason we know of," Hawk says.

"He could have said something."

"Could have."

"He didn't."

It's the end of a hot day. The night has some chill. The trees will be giving up some of their moisture soon, sending it through their roots into the ground into the cistern, but it won't be enough; every day now, especially now, we need more.

"You know that part," Hawk says, "of *Treasure Island?* Right up front, when the box arrives?"

I know that part because Hawk has told me that part, ever since he was nine years old and Dad found that pile of Scribner Classics at the county fair and brought them home for my brother, a Christmas present in September, worth hundreds and hundreds, Dad said. Hawk is a reader, a freaky good reader, and *Treasure Island* is the best book, that is what Hawk says. My brother has every word of that book in his head.

He changed his name from Junior to Hawk when he was ten, in honor of the best book in his head.

"You see it, right, Sara? How it is?"

"How what is?"

"There's a box. There's a stranger. There's a story. Gotta be."

"Hawk."

"Yeah?"

"How 'bout there's just a box. How 'bout there's just a stranger."

"More than that," Hawk says.

"Don't you be getting everything mixed up in your head. Getting everything mixed up is like lying."

He gives me a hard look.

"What?" I say.

"Who's lying?"

"I'm just saying."

"You want to know something?"

"What?"

"I'm not the liar. You think I don't know what's going on? You think I don't hear Mom and Dad talking, and you and Mom talking, and nobody talking to me? You think I don't know, Sara, about Cleveland? You think I don't know about Dr. G.?"

I look at him. I look away.

"I was going to tell you."

"When?"

"I don't know. Soon."

"Not telling is lying."

"Only sometimes."

"Not telling isn't right."

"Not telling is not the same as getting everything mixed up on purpose. And what's the point, anyway, of talking about the doctors?"

"Yeah," he says. "Right."

"Bad news is bad news, Hawk. Doesn't get any better when you tell it."

He stares at me. He shakes his head.

"What?"

"Let me introduce myself," he says. "I'm Hawk." He reaches for my hand. He shakes it. "I am your brother. When something's wrong, you have to tell me."

"Talking about my problems doesn't fix my problems. There's nothing for it, Hawk. Nothing." The words come out fast through my crowded mouth. The words are going to choke me.

Hawk lifts his Spyglass.

Sees what I can't.

Hands me the Spyglass without me grabbing.

Won't speak.

We sit in the night.

We see how dark it is.

"There's something going on in that lighthouse," Hawk says, finally. "Something like a mystery."

"Man," I say.

"What?"

"You and your stories."

"Got something better?"

"I do not."

"We keep an eye on this, Sara. Things are unfolding."

We sit. The bales of hay we never stuffed into the hay shed look like waves rolling in. I wonder what we'll do with them now. No shed for the hay. Not enough hay for the cows. Not enough of anything.

"Hawk?"

"Yeah?"

"I'm sorry."

"Yeah."

"Forgive me?"

"Maybe. This time."

He looks at me.

He smiles.

Victory Shelf

Once I was this girl and Hawk was this kid and Mom and Dad were themselves with less worries in their skin. This was before Phooey and after Old Moe. This was before I ever knew what an aortic root was, before I lay, like I am lying now, curled around my heart.

Snowed-in days were soup-making days—Dad in charge. Autumn days were pumpkin days—pumpkin pie and pumpkin seeds and pumpkin faces on the porch. Saturdays were library days—Dad, Hawk, and me in the front of the truck and up the road to County Free Library, where Mrs. Kalin lives and works, and the old newspapers and the new newspapers and the microfiche live. "Past, Present, Future at your service," she'd say, whenever we'd come in, and she'd send us home with books to read again—classics, which were Dad's style.

Once I didn't have to lie to Hawk and he didn't have to get mad at me.

I didn't have to get mad at me for not being who I want to be.

Once is a long time ago. A long time ago is long.

There's a low glow in my room, thanks to the magnitude of stars out there in the sky. The glow shines up the tractor bolts and peacock feathers on my victory shelf, the snapped half of Phooey's best egg, the clapper of the bell Dad used to ring until the whole bell cracked, an old cigar box that I once found while shoveling garden dirt. "Good as antique," Hawk said, and Mrs. Kalin, too, when we took it to her for help to guess its story.

I put our best family portraits in a box on my victory shelf—twelve of them total, one for each year of my life. The portraits are county fair work, Mabel Token in charge. She's got an old Polaroid and film, a curtain for a backdrop, a cardboard table booth, and for five dollars you can buy yourself an eternity pose; that's what she calls it. Every year since I was born the Scholls have gone to Mabel with a pose. One year just Mom and Dad and me. Every year after with Hawk.

I keep the eternity inside my box. I name each year the Year of Something. The Year of the Herd, when Dad spent his extra time on the watering trough in the cow barn. The Year of the Pigs, when Dad built the third little shack with the wood that he stripped off a cabin deep in the woods. The Year of the Goats, when Mom figured out how to make sweeter goat cheese and better goat soap and ice cream powered by Molly. The Year of Old Moe, when he caught the equine flu so bad that Hawk and I slept out in the barn beside him every night for ten straight days until he stopped coughing and kick dreaming. The Year of Mom's Apricot Meringue Pie winning the state-fair prize. Twenty-five dollars and a ribbon.

Every year is the Year of Something, the words written down on the back of the pictures Mabel took.

Dr. G. is talking to Cleveland, Mom said. Dad is talking to the banks.

Tomorrow, she meant. Dad will be talking to the banks tomorrow, during their Saturday hours. Which actually means later this afternoon, when the sun's so hot, when the cows will need some tending to, when the goats will need their second round of milking, Dad will come back home with news nobody wants. The banks never give Dad the news we want.

I hear Hawk slide his book beneath the bed. I hear the off-on on his flashlight click. I hear him puff out his pillow, and I don't move, I stay right here, curled around my heart.

"You sleeping?" Hawk asks, through the wall.

"I'm talking to you, aren't I?" I say.

The only rain that's anywhere is the rain that rains eyes to chin, over the long stretching stretch of my thinking, and now, downstairs, I hear Mom and Dad talking. I hear the number that we need: twenty grand for Sara's surgery. For the trip to Cleveland. For the family hotel stay. For the keep-it-clean stuff we'd have to buy for the house when we got home. For the parts that insurance won't pay and for the parts of the farm we'd have to pay other people to take care of when we were gone. I get up quiet, go downstairs quiet, grab the biggest flashlight from the hook on the wall, and head downstairs, into the cellar, where, if I want to cry, I can cry and nobody can hear me. If I want to pound my fists. If I want to scream.

The Seed Museum in the Cellar Might Need a Little Explaining

The cellar steps are thick with splinters and creak, but I know where to step.

The cellar is square in every direction, built like one of the cubes I learned about in my homeschool textbook. The volume of a cube is found by multiplying the length of any edge by itself twice, which means $V = a$ to the third. And I do want to cry. And I don't pound my fists.

The cellar is a cellar of preservation: one wall of jam and tomato sauce, one wall of canned peppers, peas, beans, and corn, one wall of pickled onions and cucumbers and also cabbage, and then there's my wall: Sara's Museum of Seeds.

My wall is the best wall. I take a deep breath. I take a good long look. I am not screaming.

My wall is the shelves Mom and I built when I was six. My wall is the periwinkle blue I painted when I was eight—a couple of cloud puffs painted over the blue, and a little ray of ceiling sun, just on my wall, just on my part, which Mom said was a most inspired touch. My wall is everything I've bought or found or borrowed, in my own Sara way. I got the mason jars secondhand at the county fair for a good old-fashioned steal. I got the waxy sleeves through the mail. I used to use silica-gel desiccant to help keep the seeds decent dry, but powdered milk does an excellent job, and powdered milk is cheaper. Two tablespoons of the stuff wadded up in tissue and jammed into the seed jars will do the trick; just don't forget to swap out new powdered milk for old powdered milk twice or so each year.

Don't forget a thing.

My wall is seeds—threshed and sorted, named and dated, the older seeds lined up to be planted first, because my seeds have expiration dates. Nothing lives forever.

Nothing. Nobody. Don't cry, Sara.

Seed types? You name them. I've got my self-pollinators (tomatoes and peas, especially). I've got my cross-pollinators (melons and pumpkins and squash). I've got my open-pollinators, which is mostly heirloom stuff. I've got my hybrids, which Dad calls my Grand Experiments, and which Hawk doesn't understand at all, and which, to tell the truth, are hard. I don't have a lot of hybrids, but everything deserves a chance, like one of the sayings says.

Everything. And everyone.

I keep the overhead light off and beam the flashlight on and point it to my wall. You should see my seed jars shine. You should see the peaceful quiet of seeds when they're asleep.

I wish I could sleep.

Nobody hears me crying.

Everything I Love

"Sara!" I hear Mom. "Hawk?"

Not even dawn, and I'm waiting for my dream to end, waiting for Hawk to answer Mom, but there's no sound next door. No roll out of bed, bang into clothes, click down the hallway in half-tied Docs. There's a crust of tears on the pillow beneath my cheek. Another bad dream, a bad dream that didn't end.

Doesn't end.

"Hawk?" Mom calls. "Sara!" Her voice moves from the kitchen to the bottom of the stairs. It climbs. Her flip-flops slap. Up the stairs, then down the hall. My room is first. Mom knocking. *Hawk,* I think. *Get up. Come on.* But now my doorknob turns.

"Sara," Mom says. "Breakfast."

I curl around my heart, my back to Mom. I fold my pillow to hide my tears. I tell her I'm still sleeping.

"Is that right?" she says.

"Ummm-hmmmm."

She takes a seat on the edge of my bed. I slide toward her. Don't turn.

"Sweetie," she says.

Won't open my eyes. Won't look into hers.

"I had a dream," I say. "I'm still having it."

"Who's in the dream?" she asks.

"Clevcland's in the dream. Knives. The David procedure, whoever David is."

"I know it's hard, Sara," she says. "I know it is. And I'm so sorry."

I'm scared of trying, I'm scared of not trying, I'm scared of how scared I am, I'm scared of how I didn't tell my brother the most important news there is, which is kind of a lie, and why did I lie, and why can't I just roll over and look at Mom? Why can't I ask her what will happen to the seeds I've grown and cut and threshed and jarred? Why can't I say, *Whose museum will my museum of seeds be, if we go to Cleveland, if we don't?* What if—I can't say it. I can hardly think it. What if we can't save me? What if it all comes down to the money not in the bank? The chances you don't get on a farm in drought season?

Mom digs into my covers for my hand. She puts her fingers between mine and squeezes hard.

"You know how much we love you, right?" she says. "How much I do?"

I nod.

"You know that Dr. G. is on our side."

I nod again.

"And that he's very smart."

"Yes," I whisper.

"You leave the worrying to Dad and me. You leave Dr. G. to his medicine. He's making calls, Sara. He wants to help. He knows what he's doing."

She unsqueezes my hand and combs her fingers through my hair. She sits here for a long time, then bends in close, kisses my cheek. "I'll bring you break-fast," she says. "In a little bit. Breakfast in bed. Not like we'll make that a habit."

I turn and see Mom through the blur of my tears, through the blur of hers. She looks at me for a long time, then knocks on the wall between Hawk's room and mine.

"Hawk?" she asks.

Nothing.

She knocks again.

I push myself up. The world is gooey. I look past Mom, across the room, through the window, but in the blur I don't see Hawk sitting on the pier.

"Funny," Mom says.

She leans again, knocks again, waits. She kisses me a second time and stands. She leaves my room and flip-flops down the hall to Hawk's room. Nothing. She heads back down the hall, toward my room and past it, to the stairs.

"You okay for a little bit?" she asks.

"Yeah."

She smiles thin. Flip-flops down the stairs to the door, her polka-dotted toenails vanishing. Opens the front screen door and steps onto the porch, down the plank steps. I hear her head around toward the back of the house and the tractor shed, until I can't hear her anymore.

I climb out of bed—one daddy long leg after the other.

I pull into my jeans, my yesterday shirt.

I walk in my socks to my brother's room. His *Treasure Island* is a tepee on the floor. There's a hook by the window where he hangs his Spyglass, but the Spyglass isn't there.

I grab my boots.

I wash my face.

I go flying, which for me, most of the time, when I'm not saving birds from the smoke of a fire, looks like another person walking.

Curvy Early Air

Dad's on the porch when I open the door—an egg in one hand and a hammer in his pocket. His bright-sky eyes are even more bright sky because he's standing in the sun.

He rubs the wrinkles in his brow.

I feel the curve of the early air. I feel the dream, like a wisp of smoke, inside me.

"You know what your brother's up to?" Dad asks.

I don't pretend I do. Or don't.

"Tractor's still in the shed. Goats are lonely. Cows are out on their own."

"Pigs?" I say.

"Could be the pigs. Mom's checking."

He turns to look out over the parts of the farm we can see from the porch: the dry well with the wooden bucket that Mom has planted lilacs in, the apple trees that drop their fruit, the pebble road that goes in two directions.

"I'll be back," I tell him. I clomp down the porch steps and turn up the pebbled road, and five minutes later I'm cruising around the algae pond, keeping my eye on the peahens on the deck, which are wobbling the snowflake feathers on their heads.

Beneath my feet the pebbles crunch. My boots get smoked with pebble dust.

I hike the rise to the cistern, which is like a swimming pool with a cement roof and a hatch and an aluminum ladder and a deep, deep well, and instead of decorations on the outside, there's the Magic Marker graffiti Dad wrote at the start of this drought, to remind him to remind us of the cost of doing water business:

One minute of washed hands = four gallons.

Teeth brushed with the spigot on = five gallons.

Shower longer than a song = fifty gallons.

Past the cistern is the shack, and past the shack is a buckle in the road where we sometimes find the skin of snakes left off like shiny coats. At the buckle, there's a cutaway road that slices through the woods. Up ahead there's a big square of dust and a single tree that we call the *Hispaniola*, and that's where Hawk is. I can see the loose laces of his boots swinging.

He's breathing loud. He isn't talking.

"You're missing breakfast," I tell him.

No answer.

"I could have had breakfast in bed."

Nothing.

"Mom's looking for you. Dad's looking for you. I hiked this whole hill looking for you."

"Shhhh," he says.

"What?"

"Stop talking. Climb."

I fit my feet into the crusty bark and climb. Hawk pushes the Spyglass at me before I can grab it. I dial in, and through the trees, down the hill, I see: the snow snow snow of The Mister and a big wood box busted open at his feet. There are ropes like laundry ropes crossing above his head—running from the lighthouse to a tree—and clipped to the ropes are white rectangle sheets, not sheets like bedsheets, but sheets like paper. The Mister's got a bucket in one hand, a heavy bucket, from what I see, a feed bucket, maybe, maybe a bucket from Old Moe.

"He busted the lady's box," Hawk says.

"Jeez," I say, and I feel my heart beating hard, because it looks like someone took a hammer to the thing, and that someone could only be The Mister, but that's crazy. I think of The Mister holding Phooey. I think of the splatters on his shoe shine. I think of how really old he is. You'd have to be a super mad man to bust a box like that.

"How'd you know?" I ask, handing the Spyglass back, pressing the thud of my heart with the palm of my hand. "How'd you know that he was out there?"

"Been out here on the roof since before dawn. Been watching, trying to see."

"We should tell Mom," I say, saying nothing about the crying or the dream or my own museum where I try so hard not to scream. We should tell Mom, I think, because sometimes secrets can get too big.

"Not telling Mom. Mom doesn't have to know. She's got other things to worry about."

"She should know."

"Yeah? And what would we tell her? The guy is weird is all. Mom doesn't have to know. She's got other things to worry on."

"Give me back the Spyglass," I say.

Hawk's hand through the leaves.

My hand through the leaves.

"Wait a minute," I say. Dialing in.

That box busted open. Those stones in a circle. Those white sheets still hanging in a crisscross on a line. And now The Mister is pulling the white sheets off the line. He's stuffing the sheets inside the stone circle. He's leaning down and striking a match, and a zip of red and yellow starts, a puff of smoke, more smoke, like what we need in this drought season is another fire.

"Hawk!" I say. "You see it?"

"See it!"

"We have to stop him!" I say.

I push the Spyglass back at him, start to climb down. He grabs my wrist to stop me.

"You can't *go*," Hawk says. "Remember Mom? What she said? Man wants his privacy."

"He's starting a fire! In drought season."

"Yeah. But it's staying put, inside the stones. Guy knows what he's doing. Watch."

I grab the Spyglass back and watch how, one by one, piece by piece, all the sheets of white on the criss-crossed ropes are getting yanked into the fire. Dying there. Sending up more smoke. More sheets. More flames. More smoke. All inside the stone circle.

"We're finding out what he's doing," Hawk says. "We're finding out before we tell Mom and Dad. We're not worrying them if they don't need to be worried, because they don't need to be worried. Plan?"

I hand him the Spyglass. He looks long and hard. He lists the things we already know, trying to puzzle out the story. "The Mister moves in," he says. "Lady shows up and knocks. The Mister won't answer. Lady leaves the box. The Mister busts the box. The Mister sets a fire and burns the things inside the box. The Mister says that what he needs is lots of privacy. The Mister understands fire."

"The Mister steals, too," I say. "The lawn chair. The feed bucket."

Hawk shrugs. The leaves ripple. "Stealing seems pretty minor. You think the stealing's part of this?"

"How'd I know?"

"So we keep the stealing on the list," Hawk says. "For now. Even if it might not actually matter." I can hear Hawk breathing hard. I can hear my own heart flopping. "Real-live mystery," he says. "And we're investigating."

"Sara!" We hear Dad now. "Hawk!" Dad's voice through a megaphone. Dad's voice coming up the hill.

Hawk bursts through the leaves. He jumps to the ground. The dust rises up. He's running.

"Last one to the house feeds the pigs," he calls out.

Little Santas

When Mom asks Hawk why he left ahead of breakfast without saying where he was going, he says he doesn't know; it was just an itch.

When Dad asks, he says it's because he couldn't sleep.

When Mom and Dad ask me how I knew where to find my brother, I say, "Had a hunch, is all."

When they ask us why it took so long to get back down the mountain, we say we're sorry.

Flapjacks are just as good cold as they are hot, please pass the honey. Mom watches and she doesn't talk and we eat, we eat, we eat, and now Dad shows up from the back bedroom, dressed in his idea of a suit.

The jacket's the color of denim.

The pants are burnt-orange corduroy.

The tie has little Santas on it.

"It's August," Mom says. That's all.

It's almost ten a.m. and already hot.

Mom follows Dad out of the kitchen, to the back door, then out the door to his Ford, and I can't hear what they say. The Ford revs up and pulls away and Mom calls, "I love you."

And now what? That's the question.

Shadows on the Barn Floor

Farms are full of losing. Fruit to flies, seeds to breeze, chicks to coons, fences to time, crops to drought, goats to the mistakes you make, like giving the kids too much feed, or not sterilizing the teats, or not tying the goat up tight. It's the milking hour, and the goats are bleating.

Their heads are soft.

Their friendship's easy.

I grab my buckets and my pan, the sterile wipes, my tie-in rope. I let the screen door flap behind me, watch the guinea fowls squabble at my feet, like a speckled storm cloud. The goats are high in their bleat by now, watching me walk the bridge over the dusty bed where, up until June, there was a creek. The guineas bump up into the barn and then bump back out again. They scramble in and out of my shadow.

Goats don't look to where the fire burned, to where the hay shed was, but they smell it. I try not to look, try not to think, about Dad at the bank, Dad asking questions. Dad with more to ask for now. A good face-to-face meeting can do the trick, Dad likes to say. But the banks spot a trick a mile away. They know the farmers who can't pay, the ones who are so deep into the money hole that the farm they call theirs isn't really theirs, and the cows aren't either, or the goats, or the pigs, or the house they live in. The banks always know.

The goat shack is three-sided. The fourth side is just plain weather. I set my tools down, keep my rope in hand, and call to Polly. When she doesn't come, I catch one hand inside her collar to knot the rope. She's not one for excessive fuss. She paws at me, but she doesn't mean it. I lead her to the milking post and tie her in and clean her teats and squirt her first blue milk into the pan.

When the good milk comes in, I trade the pan for the bucket. The milk hisses. Polly stomps one hoof and fixes me with her jewelry eyes. I tell her some of the trouble we're in. She's a listener. When her milk is gone, I rub her head and pull one soft ear and set her free and now I start the whole thing again, calling to Jo to come. Jo bucks Verdi the rooster out of her way with her hornless head.

I tug and the milk hisses. The sun glisten shifts. It's Molly's turn. I let Jo go and wrangle Molly. I look around and think of Mom and how, sometimes, she'll come out here in her flip-flops and a scuff of flour on her cheek and stand in the sun and look at the float of the dust of the farm. How, if I come up around beside her, she'll make me look too. She'll call it a miracle, and I'll believe her.

Dad's in his truck on the way to the bank. Mom's out by the pasture fence, fixing the hitch in the gate. Hawk is wherever Hawk is, and now Jolly pricks her ears and turns. She faces the day full on. The shadows on the barn floor change—two arms and two legs blacken the thick beam of sun.

I turn.

Nothing.

I call out, "Hey!"

I finish up with Jolly, fast, untie her. Stand and hurry from the barn, the pail of sloshing goat milk in my hand. I walk the bridge over the missing creek, walk not too fast, because if I do, I'll spill. The shadows are all gone.

"Hey," I call.

"Hey. Mister?"

But nobody answers, and the middle distance blurs.

Ridiculous Hitch

In the kitchen I pour the milk into tall glass jars, write the date on the lids with erasable ink, and put them in the cooler. I head down the long road to the trees and the pigs, and the cats come with me, good as two dogs, until they quit inside some shade. Mom's way out there on the south side fixing the gate latch, and now, closer to the Pig Village, I call Hawk's name. The pigs start running. The sunflowers swish.

"Hawk?"

No sign of my brother.

"Hawk!"

Figgis and the calico cat, Scaredy, pick themselves

up out of the shade and follow me to the house, where there's nothing I can do with the thing I thought I saw, and what I'm actually supposed to do is start lunch, because today's my turn. Shake the salt. Shake the pepper. Find the cheese. Get started.

I hear boots on the porch.

"Where've you been?" I ask Hawk.

He puts a *shhhh* finger to his lips. Makes it clear that Mom is coming, that there's news but he can't say. Something is happening. Hawk has his highest spirits on. He washes the dirt from his hands at the sink. Puts the toast in. Compliments my cooking just in time for Mom to show up and thank me with a kiss.

"Ridiculous hitch," she says as she sits down. "Rust's got the best of it."

She looks at Hawk. She looks at me.

"Dad's in town by now," she says.

We eat.

We eat.

Black Dog Goes Missing

ook off?" I say. "What do you mean?"

"Old pig shot out of the pig house like he'd been stuffed inside a cannon," Hawk says. "Headed north, straight for the loop road. Ran for the lighthouse."

I narrow my eyes. "You sure you just didn't spook him?"

"I showed up. Black Dog started running."

I sit back and give my brother another squinty stare. I shield my eyes from the sun that's falling straight through the sky, no clouds, onto us, on the pier, where it must be one hundred degrees and hotter the higher you are in the sky. I've already told my shadows-in-the-goat-shed story, and now Hawk is telling this, and I should just sit and listen, but everything Hawk says is the start of a new question.

"So you followed Black Dog," I say.

"I did."

"Couldn't help it?"

"Couldn't be helped."

"You followed Black Dog and then you saw her."

"That's what I've been saying. Right there in the flesh. High heels. Green dress. She was banging on his door, looking mad as a bug on its back. 'Seen a pig?' I asked her. Dusting off my jeans before I did. I'd pulled up easy, gave an easy hello. 'Black Dog's his name,' I said, to be specific. Lady didn't answer."

"'Course she didn't."

"She didn't even turn around."

"You were talking about a pig."

"She kept banging on the door. I thought she'd fall off of those shoes. There was heat still coming from her Rover. I asked her, 'Can I help you?' Finally she turned. She stopped."

"Looked right at you?"

"Yes. Asked me if I'd seen M.B. I said, 'Who?' She said, 'M.B.?' I said, 'You mean The Mister.' 'The Mister?' she said. 'You call him The Mister?'"

"So that's his name," I say. "M.B."

"Not much of a name, if you ask me. I asked again,

'Did you see Black Dog?' She looked at me like I was crazy."

"She didn't drive all the way here to meet some pig."

"No harm in being friendly."

I lie back on my elbows, but the tar is too hot. I sit up straight and there's the sun.

"She gave me a good look up and down," Hawk says. "She had a pocketbook hanging from her shoulder. She moved it to the other arm and watched me hard. I could tell that she was talking to herself inside, wondering if she could trust me. I stood up straight. Clapped the knees of my jeans again. Shook away the dust. I thought that might help. Respectability is the brother of trust. Just like Dad says."

"Did she? Trust you?"

"Guess she did, after a lot of looking. After a lot of thinking, too, and banging on that door some more, after calling out that name: M.B. 'Give this to your Mister,' she finally said, her voice like some surrender. 'When you see him, please do.' She handed me an envelope, this one right here. I took it. Businesslike. Trustworthy. High respectable. 'Make sure you deliver it straight to him, nobody else,' she said. 'And make sure you get an answer.' She told me not to look inside, not to tarnish up the package, not to let any curiosity get the best of me. 'Give it straight to your Mister, nobody else,' she said it again. 'Do it quick and just as soon as you can find him. Stand there while he reads it. Stand there while he answers. Can I trust you, sir, with this?' She gave me her speech, and then she gave me this. Put it into the palm of my hand." Hawk pulls a card from the pocket of his shirt. "Right here." He points. "Her name and number."

ILKE VANDERVEER. BRIGHT STAR PUBLISHING, the little blue type on the bright white card says. FLATIRON BUILDING. NEW YORK CITY. Hawk reads the whole thing out loud, the phone number, too. He raises his eyebrows. Smiles.

"She told me to call her when the mission was complete. Said there'd be a reward in it. To do it all untarnished."

"Untarnished?"

Hawk shrugs. "Her word. Just repeating."

"What kind of reward?"

"She didn't say."

"What else did she say?"

"She said The Mister was in trouble. That they're waiting in the city. That the faster he receives what I'm to deliver, the better off he will be. Also, the better off the world will be."

I gape at him. "The whole world?"

"I'm just repeating. One other thing." Hawk is so full of this that I think he'll pop. If he doesn't tell me, he'll pop. If he tells me, he'll pop. Hawk is going to blow.

"What?"

"Nobody else is allowed to know. My special delivery is a first-class secret." He stretches his arms out, even though he's sitting. He rocks forward, and I catch him.

"You're telling me."

"'Cause I tell you things. Unlike you sometimes, Sara."

"Hawk," I say. "Forget it. All right? I already said that I'm sorry."

"All right."

Hawk hands me the envelope. I turn it over. *M.B.*, it says, in spidery handwriting. The back flap is glued down. The glue is taped tight. The whole thing is wrapped with plastic thin as Saran. There's no messing with this without getting caught, no taking a peek and fixing it back up, and Hawk hasn't messed. Hawk is full of story hope. He believes in treasure.

"There's a reward," Hawk says. "If I follow instructions. Reward, maybe not your twenty grand, maybe not everything, but definitely something, which is something better than nothing. I'm doing what she asked me, Sara." And the more he talks, the more hope he shows, and the more hope he shows, the more sad I feel, because why would Hawk, my freaky-smart brother, Hawk, trust this lady and her request, and why would she trust a kid she barely met, and why is she is so desperate, anyway, and why do I have Marfan, because if I didn't, Hawk wouldn't be even dreaming of this.

"Our ship is coming in," he says.

"It's an envelope, Hawk. A single special delivery. Minor reward. Gotta be."

"Anything's possible, with a guy like The Mister. He's important, right? We know that much." He wraps his skinny arms across his skinny chest, like he can't hold everything in. He rocks again.

"He's important," I tell Hawk, give him that. "That's a definite thing."

"This is our lucky day," Hawk says. "Our actual lucky day."

"No luck in it until you make the delivery. Until he answers, and who knows how he would, or will. Answer to you? Call her up? Send a letter? This isn't good business, Hawk. This makes no sense."

"It'll make sense."

"You're too sure, Hawk."

"I'm an optimist," he says.

"No way this works," I say. "And besides, you know what Mom said. You know what she'd say if you told her."

"We won't tell them. Not until the reward is ours."

"Hawk."

"What do Mom and Dad want, Sara?" Hawk says, tilting his big eyes up at me. "What do they want *most*?"

I don't answer, but I know.

"They want the money to buy you the fix. They want the money for the shed. We surprise them with cash, they won't care about the rest of it."

"But Hawk. Seriously. You don't know what this trouble is. You don't know what it *means*."

"Can't be that hard. Doing what she wants. Right?" Hawk says, practically pleading.

"Hard isn't the point, Hawk. Hard is—"

But before I finish, I hear the churn of Dad's Ford, the white stones in a crush beneath his tires.

"Dad's back," I say.

"Yeah." Hawk nods.

I stand and Hawk stands. He slips the envelope inside his shirt and smooths down the shirt, like a regular spy.

There's bank news on the way.

Bad Math

Dad's tie is stuffed inside the pocket of his cords. His jacket hangs from the hook of his finger. He's got five o'clock shadow at the four o'clock hour, and he comes in and here we are, Mom, too, with Figgis. She lets her go and she paws around. Mom doesn't scold and I hardly breathe, because Dad hasn't said yet, because he doesn't have to say. His eyes are full of shadows. Side to side he shakes his head. Mom curses Jersey Shore words.

"Wouldn't budge," Dad explains. Mom curses again, hides the tears she has been crying behind her shades. She rubs her eyes, won't look at me, won't look anywhere near any one of us, just watches the scratched planks of the pine floor until Scaredy shows up, rubbing his affection against Mom's legs. There's a fly in a fight with the loose screen on the back door.

"Didn't like the math," Dad says. "That's what they said."

"Do they think *we* do?" Mom says, her voice like a glass bowl on its way to breaking. "Like the math?"

"'Families,' they said. 'Neighbors. Friends.'"

"What kind of friends," Mom says, "do they think we have?"

Charlotte and Jane, Mac and Mildred, Isaiah, the rest of them. We have friends, plenty. We don't have twenty grand worth of friends, and twenty grand isn't even all we need. Twenty grand is what we need for me. Leave the black smolder be. Forget the hay.

Not even a thousand people in this town. Put them all together, you wouldn't find twenty grand. Deliver the special delivery to The Mister and that is just a fraction. Twenty grand is twenty grand. The banks said no. Hawk is dreaming.

"Not remotely acceptable," Mom says, slamming her glasses back down on her nose and starting to walk the floor, scaring off Scaredy, as if walking the floor with sunglasses on will find her twenty grand. "Not even close." She'll make more pies, she's saying, more cheese. We'll sell the cows if we have to, also the pigs, but now Dad throws his jacket over the newel post and catches Mom with his big bear hands. Says "Honey," like he can save her, save us, save all this for later. Like any of us can put it aside until Hawk and I are in bed. Like there aren't already FOR SALE signs all over this town, lots of people needing to sell, signs that have vines crawling all over them, rust in the letters for all the years they've been there, trying. You don't sell. You leave. Where would we leave to? What would we have if we didn't have this? Where do you go when you disappear?

"Honey," Dad says.

"Don't," Mom says. Looking away and twisting free. The house goes still. Not even Figgis moves.

"You kids make us some fricassee," Dad says after a long moment goes by. The five o'clock shadow is creeping up in his eyes. He goes after Mom and the door slams hard. He calls her name, and now he's running.

The door slams again. It's Hawk this time. Running north to the lighthouse, with his special delivery tucked tight against his chest.

You kids make us some fricassee.

You kids is me.

Fryers

Three pounds of fryers, cutup. One and a half cups of pitted prunes. Two cups of broth and some salt, and some gingerroot, and some brown sugar and cinnamon and water. You coat the chicken. You brown the meat. You fire up the Dutch oven. Everything else is what comes next. Reduce the heat and cover. Keep the gas low until the chicken cuts are tender and stand there, steaming yourself, pretending the tears that you cry are not tears and that your brother isn't out there believing the impossible is true, and that your mom and dad aren't down the road talking it out, in anger and in private, and that you alone aren't the cause of this; you are the cause of it.

Didn't like the math, is what the bankers said.

Math has a name. Math's name is Sara.

Awake

"S ara," Hawk whisper-talks. "You awake?"

His window scrapes up and back down. He presses his face to my piece of glass. The whole house smells like the fricassee no one wanted and some of the smoke left over from the fire. There's a nighttime chill in the heat.

"I'm coming," I say.

Get up from the bed. Walk the floor. Climb.

Hawk's got his Spyglass out and his feet kicking. The lights of Dad's Ford are on up on the cistern hill, sending raking yellow beams down and past the pond and across the first hem of the field.

"I knocked," Hawk says. I kick my feet too. I kick the night into pure bruising. "I knocked off half my knuckles. No answer from The Mister."

Hawk lifts his fist for proof of the hard knocks, and I see the Band-Aids from the fire. I see the roughed-up parts of his knuckles.

"She said to hand it to him personal," Hawk continues. "Hand it to him. No tarnish. Quick as you can. But he doesn't want whatever it is."

"What could be so bad that The Mister wouldn't want it?"

"Plenty of things."

"Any books you ever read that bad, Hawk?"

"None that I ever finished."

He turns to his right, where the envelope sits, and grabs it. He puts it on my lap. It has no more weight than the wing of a small bird. Seems like it could be nothing at all, except for all the glue and plastic.

"You think this could really be worth something?" I ask.

"Worth hoping for," Hawk says. "Isn't it? And it's simple enough, or it should be, anyhow: Get the letter into his hands, untarnished. Get the reward."

"I guess yes. If the lady is serious."

"If you'd have seen her, you'd have seen: she was serious."

"Okay."

Hawk waits a beat. Then: "There's more."

"What's more?"

"This." Hawk reaches to his right again, rustles something new onto his lap. Not enough stars to see it by, but I smell the vague whiff of dark smoke. Hawk passes it to me. A piece of paper.

Three pieces. Three pieces of thick paper, with torn, rough edges.

"Found them floating around," Hawk says. "By the lighthouse. When I went to knock. Maybe they flew away before he bonfired the rest. Or"—and now he drops his voice low—"maybe he left them out on purpose."

"I don't—" I stop. Something shivers up through me. Like it's brittle cold out here, but it's not like that. I see Dad's headlights glow out there in the woods. I feel it, more than see it.

"Pieces of paper with words on them, more like," Hawk says, still whispering. "Instructions, it seems. Handwritten. 'Retreat,' is what it says on one. 'Relinquish.' 'Surrender.' Each piece with one word on it."

"What's it mean?"

"Heck if I know."

"What would it mean if it were in one of your books?"

"It's never been in one of my books."

I fix the old facts in with the new ones. I put them into order. A man shows up. A woman follows. A box is smashed. A bonfire flames. There's a letter wrapped in plastic that the man it's for won't read. There are three white flags with words on them. *Retreat. Relinquish. Surrender.*

"This story is a classic," Hawk says, nodding. "Classic stuff."

"But what's it mean?" I'm rocking forward now, edge of this roof. I'm rocking and Hawk catches me, and we've got no good answers, neither one of us. All we've got is questions: Who is The Mister? Who is Ilke Vanderveer? What is Bright Star Publishing? What is the size of the reward? Why would she even pretend there is a reward? Why would she give some Topflight Secret Mission to my brother, a perfect stranger so far as Ilke is concerned? Now on the hill, Dad's truck is coming back. He cuts the engine. The world is dark except for firefly freckles, and everything is silent.

"We need more facts," Hawk says, and I can barely hear him now. "There's something The Mister's afraid of, for sure."

"Can't be afraid of you, Hawk. Nobody's afraid of you."

"Maybe," he says, lying back under the stars.

"Maybe what?"

"Maybe we take the facts to Mrs. Kalin at the library. We tell her what we know."

"Yeah," I say. "But then—" *Privacy,* I think. Mom's rules. Making trouble where we don't need more trouble.

"You have a better plan?"

I shake my head.

"You think we have time to lose?"

"I don't."

"All we do is go to the library," Hawk says. Shooting up now, sitting straight, his eyes huge and happy with his plan. "All we do is say, 'Hey, Mrs. Kalin.' No harm in it. Can't be." He lifts his knocked-raw knuckles with his fire Band-Aids for a high five and I high-five. Across the field, the lighthouse suddenly beams. Turns itself on like it has been listening.

"Hello, Mister," Hawk says, training his Spyglass on the spectacle. He doesn't move. I barely hear him breathe.

"Anything?" I finally ask.

He hands me the Spyglass. He waits. I dial in and out. Refine my seeing through my glasses through the two brass barrels. Find The Mister going round and round on the top floor of the lighthouse, his white hair like dandelion gone to seed.

"Why does he do that?" I ask.

"Why would anyone?"

"Like something's chasing him. But what? Who?"

I hand the Spyglass back to Hawk. I watch the white head blur and whirl.

"We'll tell it to Mrs. Kalin," I say.

"Some of it," Hawk says. "Not all."

"Enough of it," I say, "to get good answers."

Good Day for a Getaway

I don't know if Hawk slept. I sure as anything didn't. I've been lying here and now I'm up listening to Hawk tiptoeing downstairs with his industrial-size flashlight. He'll take care of the pigs before the sun comes up. I'll work the garden, too—my Pathfinder beanie throwing yellow cones across the rows like a Hollywood set. Moisture creeps up from the earth at this hour. Spiders web to catch the dew. I'll pull the weeds, I'll pluck the bugs, I'll fill my basket with the ripe stuff, I'll set the mesh fences back into their proper attitudes to stop the coons that would otherwise come scratching.

I'm up.

I go down.

I head outside.

I work.

Phooey keeps her distance. The peahens are white lights.

"Everything early," Hawk had said through the wall last night. "Morning chores done before morning."

It's a good day for a getaway. Mom and Dad have plans of their own. Neighbors they'll go to see. Friends like Charlotte and Jane and Mac and Mildred and the ones who live close and the ones who live far and some people in the fire brigade. I heard them talking. "No harm in asking," Mom said, and Dad said, "You know they would help if they could, but honey: they're stuck in this drought same as us."

You can put your cows up for sale, your pigs, your goats, your land, even, the house you built out of a barn, the double-wide oven where your pies fluff up, but if nobody is buying, what good is the sale? If nobody has, what good is asking? "Honey," Dad kept saying, but Mom wasn't listening. Mom can't.

Hawk got his stories from Dad. He got his stubborn from Mom.

I got my Marfan from nobody.

I'm so mad at my Marfan. I'm just so mad.

Dad's on his early chores. He sees my lit-up beanie. He pulls his Ford to the end of my row. He cuts the beams, but leaves the engine running.

"Early bird catching the worms?" he asks, leaning out of the pickup window.

"Couldn't sleep," I tell him, standing up out of my crouch and watching my shadow run its length down the row beneath the twin lights on my beanie, toward the place the hay shed was.

"Your brother got a case of the couldn't sleeps too? Mighty early for pigs, wouldn't you say?"

"Maybe," I tell him.

"Curiouser and curiouser," Dad says. Scratching the beard he didn't shave.

He looks up at the sky, where the moon still shines, though the night is growing more pale. I can feel him looking for words to say that I wish he didn't have to look for.

"Dad?"

"Ma'am?"

"What's the story on The Mister?"

"The Mister's our tenant," he says. Matter-of-fact. "Two months' rent up front. Five hundred dollars each month after. Best crop we have."

"But the secrets," I say. "What's with that?"

"What kind of secrets?"

"The don't-talk-to-him-unless-he-talks-to-us parts.

The don't-even-take-him-a-slice-of-Peach-Marshmallow parts. Seems to me he's missing out."

"You're all lit up with shine," Dad says.

"What do you mean?"

"That hat, for one thing. That concern for The Mister."

"Just asking, Dad."

"Lots to be asking after," Dad says. "Like you out here in the dark with your greens. And Hawk up the road with the pigs. Not even a crack of sun out here."

Desperate times call for desperate measures, I almost say, quoting Dad from the framed words, but I hold my tongue. I don't need to be raising any suspicions, don't need Dad asking questions, don't need him worrying any more than he is. Hawk and I have our plan, and if I told Dad now about the box, the smash, the fire, the letter, the Ilke from New York City, the letters *M* and *B*—if I told Dad about our spying at night, Dad could shut us down.

Mess up The Mister's trust, we lose the crop we have.

Mess up Hawk's plan for the big reward that may not be big, but it could, and we won't have a single hope at paying for the David.

"Eggplants have come in nice," I say. "Plenty of plump to them."

"Welcome news."

"Saw a cloud," I said. "Last night. Over the moon."

Dad looks up toward the sky, which is growing grayer now. All the wisps are gone.

"Could be a sign," Dad says, but he doesn't mean it. He turns the headlights back on. He three-point turns. He stops. Sits in the cab of his Ford, deciding.

"You up to something, Sara?" he asks.

"Just picking," I say, which isn't a lie because right this minute that's what I'm doing. Through the dawn, with the beams, I see him watching. I know he wants to ask me more. I know that he won't. Hard enough being me, with this news. Why make it even worse, with questions?

"Breakfast at seven," he says. "Sharp. You make sure to tell your brother."

"Sir," I say.

The Ford shifts.

Farmer Speed

The air is the color of an old sock. We walk. Hawk and me, with our farmer speed, and our eyes checking over our shoulders for shadows. Ruckus, Mac's dog, has chased Mom and Dad in their truck, barking a storm up the yellow divider line. He'll follow them halfway, and then he'll quit—lope back home down the middle of the road with his tongue hanging out. He'll lie in the shade waiting for them to return.

"You're on your own for lunch," they said, Mom all dressed up, her best boots on, an iron crease in each cotton sleeve. Dad wearing that denim jacket and jeans, no Santa Claus tie, no cap.

They had their worry on.

They waved goodbye.

I held Scaredy and Figgis, one in each arm, but now they're gone, and Hawk and I have the morning. Plus.

Through the shade of the green trees, we walk. Past the cows to our right and the pigs to our left. At the curve in the road, Hawk pulls his whistle from his pocket and blows. The pigs all turn to squealers and Hawk laughs, first time I've heard him laugh in a really long time now. By the time we reach the start of Mountain Dale, Isaiah is there with his horse and buggy. That horse, by the way, is Spots.

"I'm calling in favors," Hawk says. He hollers Isaiah's name. He runs.

Hawk makes room for me on the buggy's back ledge. I fold myself in and sit, my knees up to my chin.

"And a good morning to you," Isaiah says, exaggerating his civility, like he does, not asking about the fire because that's also protocol. Help where help is needed. Don't rub the bad news into anybody's eyes. If we want to talk fire, Hawk and I will talk fire. We don't want to, so we don't.

Isaiah tips his hat and talks to Spots. We head off to what some people around here call a town, and what Hawk calls a hamlet, and what I say is a couple of buildings and a playground and a big patch of dried-up earth where they run the Bean Festival and County

Fair every year, come September. Also a pool for the veterans' crowd, but there being a drought, the pool's closed. We hit the intersection where the Minute Market is, and pick up speed on the down part of the hill where, early in June, a semi lost control of itself and took out the Pizza Palace, and all this time Hawk is leaning close to the brim of Isaiah's hat, getting news from Isaiah's lay of the land.

Lost a cow to cancer eye.

Lost a pair of ducks to a fox.

Horse got loose, but then it came back, hungry for hay and attention.

Father Cole is bent on a new crop of pumpkins.

"What do you need the library for?" I hear Isaiah ask now. "Don't you have all those Scribners?"

Everybody who is a friend of Hawk's knows something about those Scribners.

"Family business," Hawk says.

Isaiah whistles. A semi whishes by. Spots canters off to one side, tips his head like he does to the rude ones. When the dust settles, Spots starts trotting again. When we get to the main highway, which is just a two-lane highway, he waits to cross until Isaiah gives him the sign. We buggy into town behind a silver Prius that looks a little dazed; must be a tourist driving that thing.

There's a redbrick rancher beside the white post office. The two things share a droopy flag. We stop.

This is it. Our library. One room for books. One room for Mrs. Kalin. Her housing comes with the job.

Spots gets a good giddy-ho from Isaiah. Hawk hops out. I follow, but not as fast. Both feet on the ground, I let a case of dizziness pass. Hawk promises Isaiah a slice of future pie.

"You tell Rayuda it's on me," Hawk says.

"Planning to," Isaiah says.

The painted sign on the screen door says the library opens at ten, but Mrs. Kalin keeps farmer hours. She's out watering the window boxes when we arrive. Sets her can down near the stone wargs and orcs and Elven-birds that gather round on the burnt-out lawn. Direct descendents of J. R. R. Tolkien, she'll tell anyone, and not a buccaneer in the bunch.

Hawk likes her despite.

She's wearing a flowered dress with a wide black belt and little slipper shoes. Every year at the fair parade, Best Dressed goes to her, partly on account of the hats she builds out of the pages of recycled books. Even people who don't read come to the library to see those hats, which she hangs from hooks and invisible strings from the library's two crisscrossing wooden beams.

There's year after year of paper hats hanging in that air—the Robin Hood hat, the Madeline hat, the Quangle Wangle hat, the Thing One hat.

There's a circulator fan on the windowsill. When it blows its air at the hanging hats, they do a little waltz.

She follows us in. Wipes sweat from her brow. Asks what she can do for us. Hawk stands square on his Doc Martens boots. He says we have a research project. We are in need of facts.

"You've come to the right place," Mrs. Kalin says. "Specifically which facts?" she asks. She knows about the fire, too. She knows the protocol. She doesn't ask.

She cleans her hands with sanitizer. She fixes the belt on her dress. Beneath the dangling paper hats, the books sit on shelves arranged like a backward capital *E*. There's a long table between the first two arms of the *E* and two side-by-side computers. There are carts of periodicals you can push around on wheels.

"We have a situation," Hawk finally says.

"We have to keep it confidential," I chime in.

"A confidential situation," Mrs. Kalin says. Her forehead frowns. Her mouth smiles. She fits her clean hands on her hips.

Hawk pulls the card with the blue type from the pocket of his pants. He sets it square on the long table. Mrs. Kalin pulls glasses from the top of her head down to the bridge of her nose.

"Ilke Vandervecr," she continues. "Bright Star Publishing. Flatiron Building.

"Where in the world," she continues, with her quiet voice, a voice that whispers most of the time because it lives next door to books, "did you get this?"

Looking from Hawk to me and back to Hawk. Hawk shrugs. I answer. I wish we had rehearsed this.

"She gave it to Hawk."

"Ilke herself?" Mrs. Kalin asks me. She shakes her head.

"I'd lost my pig," Hawk offers. "Black Dog."

"You lost your pig," Mrs. Kalin repeats. "So you got this." She tries to follow, but she's lost. I start the story closer to its start. "We've got a renter," I say. "In the old corn silo. Dad turned it into a house. A three-room house. One room on top of the other. With windows on top. And a spiral stairs in the middle, and—"

Hawk interrupts. "Guy showed up a few weeks ago. Moved in. Old man. Then she showed up. Ilke Vanderveer. And she gave me her card."

Mrs. Kalin's eyes go from one of us to the other.

We haven't mentioned the crate or the special delivery with its plastic wrap. We've been good on the step by step. We've been careful, watching ourselves, and Mrs. Kalin is watching us, reading us, it feels like to me, like we were some of her books.

Raise no suspicions.

Cast no doubts.

"Who is Ilke Vanderveer?" I ask, because something's

up; Mrs. Kalin knows. The name has hit her like a thud.

"Well, I've never met her myself," Mrs. Kalin says. "I can't imagine that many small-town librarians have." She pulls out a chair at the table and sits. Hawk and I sit. It smells like books in here. Mrs. Kalin folds and unfolds the hem of her flower skirt. She decides what she should tell us.

"Ilke Vanderveer is an editor," she says now. "She's launched some of the world's most famous books."

"Launched," Hawk repeats, liking the ship shape of the word, I can tell. *Treasure Island* stuff.

"Makes books happen," Mrs. Kalin explains. "Sends them out into the world." When she says it, I see the Elven-birds at work, stitching pages together with their golden beaks and dropping them onto doorsteps with their golden feet.

"So who is M.B.?" Hawk asks.

Mrs. Kalin gives us a blank, then a startled stare. Like she didn't know and now she does and now she can't believe it.

"What do you know about M.B.?" she asks.

"That he's renting from us," I say. "That he's ancient." *Snow snow snow,* I think, don't say it. Red-shine shoes and splatter. I don't say about the shadows he makes. I don't say about his unicycle rides. I don't say that the only time we've good-and-proper met him, he was the gentlest old guy I've ever seen, holding Phooey in his hands, shy. Handing Phooey over and not wanting dinner.

Mrs. Kalin closes her eyes to think. I see her eyeballs fluttering beneath her lids and now the flutter stops. She pushes back in her plastic chair, stands up, pushes a cart to one side, goes behind her desk, powers on her computer. It hums. She taps. Waits. Takes two steps to where the printer is and waits some more for something to roll through.

All this time, Hawk and I are sitting.

Waiting.

My dizziness returns.

We're telling secrets we shouldn't have told.

We've left the farm with no one in charge.

Leaving the farm like this is a kind of sin.

Telling secrets is a kind of sin, too.

"Just as I thought," Mrs. Kalin says now, walking to us with the pages in hand, reading them out loud. "M.B. Martin Bruce Banks. Author/illustrator of the Roundabouts series. A Bright Star superstar. Gone missing."

"Author!" Hawk says.

"Superstar!" I say.

"Gone missing," Mrs. Kalin repeats herself. And now we stay quiet so she can explain. She lays the pages down before us. We lean in close to read. "Here it is," she says. "A bit of a mess, if you ask me."

Five different headlines. Each one says practically the exact same thing, except for the parts that are different:

M. B. BANKS, MAGICAL MIND BEHIND
THE ROUNDABOUTS, FAILS TO DELIVER
LAST BOOK IN TRILOGY
(*Publishers Weekly*)

WHERE IS M. B. BANKS?
HALF A MILLION READERS EAGER
TO FINISH THE STORY
(*The Horn Book Magazine*)

ILKE VANDERVEER PRESSED TO
EXPLAIN THE DISAPPEARANCE OF
FAMED ILLUSTRATOR M. B. BANKS
(*Shelf Awareness*)

SCHOOL CHILDREN CAMPAIGN TO
RETURN M. B. BANKS TO HIS TRILOGY
(*Booklist*)

RED SHOES CREATOR LEAVES HIS
READERS ON A CLIFF
(*The New York Times*)

"You've never read the Roundabouts, have you?" Mrs. Kalin says.

Hawk and I shake our heads no.

"Half a million copies in print," she says. "Half a million waiting for the end of a story. Modern classics,"

Mrs. Kalin says, as if it just occurs to her now why we kids are so in the dark.

She walks to the other side of the backward *E*. She returns at once, the paper hats waltzing when the fan rotates and blows. She hands a book to Hawk and a book to me.

"*Roundabouts: Book Two*," she says. "*Roundabouts: Book One*."

I open my book. Hawk opens his. It's the most beautiful thing I've ever seen. Mountains in a float of clouds. Daffodils for teacups. Grass grown tall as fences. Dogs asleep on four-poster beds. Every picture like it was drawn underwater, with a leaking pen and a multicolor brush, and in every picture there's a pair of red shoes. It's just a book of pictures, no words.

Don't need those words.

"How long has it been, Sara, since you visited me here?" Mrs. Kalin asks.

"Three years?"

"Sounds about right. Three years. *Book One* of the Roundabouts came out four years ago, and we got our copy here a year after that; pending the county auction, pending our new-book fund. *Book Two* debuted the year after that; showed up here six months ago. *Book Three* has been promised again and again. And then M. B. Banks went missing. And when he went missing, Ilke Vanderveer was put into a bad spot."

"Bad spot?" Hawk asks.

"A manner of speaking," Mrs. Kalin said. "She's the most powerful editor in all of New York. Kids and teachers and librarians and parents are waiting on her to deliver."

"How can she deliver what somebody else is supposed to make?" I ask.

"Precisely," Mrs. Kalin says. "She can't. Only thing she can do is ask and hope and wait."

"And ask him again," I say. "I guess."

"She can ask him," Mrs. Kalin says. "But he'll have to cooperate. He's the only one with the imagination. The only one with the story."

"And if he doesn't?" Hawk says. "Cooperate?"

"From the sound of the story you've just told, that's the situation we're in."

"A confidential situation," I say, for emphasis.

"Confidential," Mrs. Kalin says, but she doesn't look so sure now. She looks a little sick, to be honest. A little sick, and a little excited, both things at the same time. She doesn't push us to say more than we already have. She doesn't say anything herself, and then she does.

"You don't rush art," she says. "You cannot demand it. Mountain Dale is a pretty enough place, a small enough place, for a story maker to take a break."

"But the thing is," Hawk says, the worry in his

eyebrows now, "the thing is Ilke Vanderveer has found him." And now he talks, flushed and fast, about all the stories that he loves and how each one is its own best thing and each one was made by a hero of his and that the people who write should be the heroes. "The people who write"—and now he's searching for a word—"should be protected," he says. "The people who write—the people who could tell stories *without* words—shouldn't be forced to cooperate."

Especially by him, he doesn't say. Especially by Hawk himself, who for a little while there was on Ilke Vanderveer's side, all for the sake of—me. All because of—Marfan.

"And for some reason," Mrs. Kalin says, fishing, "Ilke Vanderveer has given you her card."

"A just-in-case scenario," Hawk says, trying to back out of the truth now, I see it.

"Just in case what?" Mrs. Kalin asks.

"Just in case . . . I don't know," Hawk stumbles.

He looks at me.

I look at him.

I check the clock.

I stand up quick, like all of a sudden I remember some appointment.

"Wow," I say. "It's getting late. We promised Mom and Dad—"

"Yeah," Hawk says. "Mom and Dad."

"Promised them we'd be back."

"I think there's more to this story," Mrs. Kalin says.

Hawk nods. Then he shakes his head. The opposite of any kind of answer.

"You'll keep in touch?"

"We'll keep in touch."

"You sure you can't stay?"

"Can't."

"How are you getting back?"

"Good day for a walk," Hawk says.

"No," Mrs. Kalin says. "I'll drive you."

"No thank you," Hawk says, quick, his voice like a hiccup.

"No point in it," I double up.

"Here," Mrs. Kalin says. She takes the *Roundabouts: Books One* and *Two*, out of our hands, slips the due-date cards from their backs, walks to her desk, and stamps them. "Three weeks," she says, "and then you two bring those books back. Library fines," she warns, "if you don't."

"Thank you, Mrs. Kalin."

"Three weeks," she says. "And you'll come back."

"Three weeks," I say. "We promise."

She follows us to the door. She heads outside behind us. She picks up her watering can to finish off the flowers and stands there watching us.

The day is hotter than it was.

There's not a ripple in the flag.

It's a long trek back.

"You sure you don't want a ride?" she says.

"Sure," Hawk says.

I feel Mrs. Kalin's eyes on us.

I feel the weight of *Roundabouts* in my hand.

The beauty of a story that doesn't have a single single word.

The strangeness of the man who won't give up the ending. A famous man. Who lives with us. Who swirls around on his unicycle in a lighthouse room and follows me like he's my shadow and won't answer the door when my brother knocks and who burns things, but not all things, and who is, still, except for when you minus out the parts we know, a total mystery.

Retreat.

Relinquish.

Surrender.

And Hawk is thinking: *Don't.*

Nobody Should Be Forced into an Ending

This long walk on this long day is the thump, is the thump of my heart. It is the sun, it is the sun, it is the sun. It is the hills that go down and the hills that go up and the rounding of the road with the low side ditch that you have to jump into when the cars and the trucks go zoom, and then, after they zoom, you climb back out, you catch your breath, you have to keep on walking.

My brother is only walking, he's not talking. My brother is completely silent.

It's so hot out here.

The farm is far.

"Could you talk?" I finally ask.

"Not talking," Hawk says. He kicks a loose stone with the toe of his boot.

"Could you tell me what you're thinking?"

He doesn't say no. He doesn't say yes. He just keeps walking.

"Hawk?"

"Okay," he says.

I wait.

"Hawk?" I have to remind him.

"Cooperate." He chews the word.

"Cooperate." When I say it, I spit it.

"I'm an idiot," he says. "I'd thought it all through—I thought The Mister could help us—but he's in a pickle too."

"You didn't have time to think."

"*You* knew."

"'Cause I'm older, Hawk."

"Shut up. You're not that much older."

"'Cause I know some things that you don't know."

"Yeah. Well. You don't know everything."

He turns and walks backward so I can't see his face. I can still see his arm, his fist, that reaches up to blot his crying.

"Hawk—"

He turns and walks the right way again. He gets quieter and quieter, a super-sad kind of quiet, and I feel sick inside, like I swallowed a cloud. A heavy rain cloud. A black one.

We walk and we don't talk. We walk and we walk and we walk.

He kicks another stone. He kicks another one. He shifts his book from hand to hand. We walk, completely silent. If I could, I would find a patch of corn or a patch of hay or a row of hairy asparagus and crawl inside. If I could, I would take a long lie-down in the shade and open my borrowed *Book One* and turn and keep turning the pages and forget everything except for those red, red shoes. I would tell the bugs and bees and the crows and hawks and the snakes and mice that in this very place someone very famous lives, someone who is looking for an ending, and then I would turn this book into a pillow for my head and close my eyes and sleep through the dusk and the stars and the moon and when I woke up, everyone who is wishing for a best or better ending would have found their best or better ending. Everyone would have a pair of red shoes that takes them just precisely where they most want to go.

"Hawk?" I say, but he doesn't look up.

Chickens and Eggs

Jerry Saunders of Chickens and Eggs slows on the road in his lemon-colored pickup with its one wood-paneled door. "Need a lift?" he asks.

Hawk and I nod.

"Good day?" Jerry asks, as we climb into the back.

Hawk nods again. I say, "Yes, sir," like a Scholl should, or would, if she weren't all caught up in an endings mystery.

We ride the rest of the way home in the pickup crib, Hawk's nose deep in *Book Two* and me holding *Book One* against my chest. We bump over the carriage-wheel ruts and slide on the turns and brace ourselves on the downhill slopes, and the cows and the horses and the dogs out there never notice us, don't look up.

At the edge of our drive, Jerry pulls up hard and we jolt back. We stand, we jump, we thank Jerry for the ride and he strokes his beard, clicks his dirty thumbnail on his overall strap.

"Offering my condolences," he says. "About the fire."

"Sir."

"Was downtown myself when the thing started. Would have come," he says. "You tell your parents."

"Sir," Hawk repeats.

"You have a good day," I say.

Hawk and I walk. Him holding his book. Me holding mine.

"M. B. Banks," Hawk says, looking toward the lighthouse.

"Who'd have guessed it?" I say, because who would have?

Hawk thumbs through the book in his hand. I see the colors going by, pages that look wet, like they were just drawn.

"This is so much bigger than we thought," Hawk says, quiet, like the pigs might hear.

He keeps thumbing his book. He stops at a page of saturated color, touches a finger to it. I think about all the times I've seen him reading his Scribners, how much he loves his stories, how much he appreciates the people who make them, the people who should be perfectly free to come up with their own endings.

"Maybe we're looking at this all wrong," I say.

Hawk glances up.

"Maybe we could actually help The Mister." It's a small part of an idea, just a beginning.

"I don't see how."

"We'd need more information," I say, "before we can know for sure."

"Mrs. Kalin already told us everything," Hawk says. "We can't help Ilke, so we can't help you, and that is the end of the story."

"That doesn't have to be the end," I insist. "It actually and truly doesn't."

Hawk looks up at me, my shadow throwing a skinny long line past his feet. I see the start of a smile on his lips. "So," he says, "what's the end?"

"I'm thinking."

"Thinking what?"

"I'm not done thinking yet."

"Sara?"

"Pigs need you," I say. He looks from me to the pigs. He looks back again.

"Sara?"

"Time for chores," I say.

He stares for a good long time. His face changes, it

keeps changing. He looks this side of proud of me, and I let him be proud, even though and actually, I don't have a verified plan. He tucks *Book Two* under his arm and shrugs a shrug and leaves the road and heads for the pigs. They squeal for him, don't quit squealing.

"Lunch at the house when you're done with the pigs," I call.

"Yeah," he says. "Better be *de*lish."

What I Would Say If I Could

I place the slices of bread in a line across the kitchen counter—seven white squares. I spread the peanut butter first and after that Charlotte and Jane's preserves, then lay another seven white squares down on top, even things up, make things nice. I halve the sandwiches on the diagonal. I take a frozen can of lemonade out, reach for a pitcher, slice an orange, add some ice cubes, and lunch will be served, soon as Mom and Dad get home.

Lunch will be served, middle of the afternoon now, whenever they get home from asking people with broken fences and ornery cows and drought conditions for more of what they don't have. Whenever they get done asking for their own best or better ending. I've got a plan, a plan's coming. Mom and Dad are still gone and Hawk is out with the pigs and I've checked on the goats and Phooey and Old Moe. I've sat on the porch, watching the low pond to one side and the hayfield to the other and the silo over there, across the way. I've carried *Roundabouts* from each place to place, and I've thought of all the things that I might say if a shadow came around and showed itself and started talking like a man.

Those are some beautiful drawings, I'd say.
That's some pair of red shoes.
That's some imagination.
That's some kind of beautiful.
That's some adventure to go on.

Nobody Talks About It

Mom and Dad say *luscious* about the sandwiches and *great* about the orange slices, and they sit here chewing. Passing the pitcher back and forth. Spooning the orange out of the bottom and breaking the rinds with their teeth. The juice is running down Dad's hands and Mom just lets it. She doesn't say, *How about a napkin?* like she always says, and it's three in the afternoon, and "luscious" is not a word you use for a PB&J, fancy sliced or not.

Nobody talks. Nobody says anything about where they've been, what step or what steps have been taken.

The house is as quiet as a house can be when four people are chewing and drinking.

"How are you feeling?" Mom finally asks me.

"Fine," I say.

"You need to rest," she says. "You were up early."

"I'll take some of that rest myself," Hawk says. "If you're giving rest out."

Mom and Dad exchange looks. Dad wipes his sticky hands. "I'll pick up your chores," he says. "You both have the afternoon off."

Nobody around here gets the whole afternoon off, except for me sometimes. It's a very negative sign. Hawk doesn't fight it.

I finish my sandwich and the last of the lemonade and head upstairs. Hawk follows.

"The *Hispaniola*," I say, when we've gone past where they can hear. "Thirty minutes."

"This your plan?" He has a wink in his voice.

"Thirty minutes," I say. Then I shut my door and lie down on my bed, digging *Roundabouts: Book One*, out from beneath my pillow, where I thought to hide it before I went all luscious with the lunch. I close my eyes so I can think. I go round and around, like a mental unicycle, until I land inside a memory that might also be a dream. I am very small and my feet are tiny. I have red shoes on. I am running. Nobody knows that I've got this Marfan thing yet. Nobody knows, and that is why it's such a great beginning.

"Sara!"

A knock at my door. Hawk's whisper.

"I don't think—" he starts to say.

"You're not doing the thinking," I say, rolling up off the bed, opening the door.

"Sara—" He looks at me hard, good and plenty.

"We'll need some stuff," I say.

He's listening.

Stealth Operation

We leave our bedroom doors closed so Mom and Dad will think we're sleeping and we tiptoe out soon as Hawk gives the all clear. Mom's working that broken fence again. Dad is out with the pigs. They're ignoring the fire scorch. They can't see us because they're not looking.

Walk.

Hurry.

Half run.

Up the hill, past the cistern, down the path to the *Hispaniola*, me with *Book One* in my hands, Hawk with his Spyglass and the special delivery, a whistle around his neck, won it at the county fair, four years ago. Quickest corn shucker in the under-tens.

I'd told him to bring it, plus the delivery. He'd asked me what for. Now I'm telling him the plan and his eyes are bigger than the biggest planets, and it doesn't hurt so much in my heart.

"Soon as we spy The Mister heading out for a walk, you go running," I tell Hawk, who has climbed high into the tree. "You'll get to where he is and stop. You'll walk by like it's just coincidence. You'll offer him up a tour of the farm. 'Hey, you want to meet my pigs?' you'll say."

"I'm saying that?" Hawk says. "Just like you said it?" He sticks his head between the leaves of the tree and looks at me like I'm crazy. And also like he likes it when I'm crazy. And also like lately I've not been crazy enough. A lot of things are blurry. But I see my brother, Hawk.

"Soon as you and The Mister are out of sight," I say, "I'll head down the hill myself, through the field, to the lighthouse. I'll see what I can see. I'll be the clue collector."

"Clue collector." Hawk snorts.

"I'm an excellent clue collector," I say, to shut him up, but he's almost laughing.

"What's so funny?" I say.

"You," he says. "Like this."

"Just go down there," I tell him. "And distract him."

"Got it."

"You'll have the special delivery with you. If you need to, you can talk about that."

"I don't need props for talking," Hawk says.

"Just in case," I say, "you can say, 'That lady, Ilke— she was around. That lady, she brought this.' You can say that you didn't like the lady much, that straight off you didn't trust her, you were just minding your own business, and she gave you something, and you just wanted him to know, in case it mattered."

"Man," Hawk says. "You should be writing books."

"Point is: we're not helping Ilke. Point is: your job is distraction. Point is: we're doing this for him, not her, which is basically like we're doing it for us."

"Minus the reward."

"Yeah. Right."

"I get your points."

"Good. Once I've got the all clear, I'll go down and look around," I continue. "When you're on your way back, blow that whistle around your neck. If The Mister asks why, just say, easy enough, that the whistle is bird talk, a necessary aid in herding the birds, including our own Phooey. 'Remember Phooey?' you'll say."

"Sara."

"What?"

"I'm not saying, 'Remember Phooey.' I do know how to talk."

"True, you do. As soon as you blow the whistle, I'll run."

"Fast as you can," Hawk says, giving me the look.

"I can run," I say. "When I have to."

"Not too fast," Hawk says, like he's Mom or Dad or the doctor. Like I'm not in charge.

I'm in charge.

"We're doing what we have to. Both of us."

"I distract," Hawk repeats the plan. "You look around. Then run."

"Right."

It's hot but there's a swell of breeze. I watch the lighthouse, the blur of it, and think of the day Dad came to dinner with his grand scheme—the silo conversion scheme plan, he called it.

Proud.

"All we need is a little ingenuity," Dad said that day.

"You're going to need more than that," Mom said, not so sure and passing the butter, filling our glasses, offering us seconds, but this time Dad was right. This time Dad didn't need much of a loan and the lighthouse opened for business, and anyone driving down Mountain Dale Road might see a farm in the fix of a drought, but not Hawk and me, not anymore. We see a story.

Beginnings. Endings.

Hawk's bootlaces tick. I'm turning the pages of *Book One*, slow and nice, following that pair of red shoes through the watercolor drips and shadows. Star of this book is these red shiny shoes that are trekking and stopping and finding and hiding, going all around The Mister's made-up world, which is the prettiest world I've ever seen, a happy place, a place where no one worries.

The shoes are riding the wings of a hawk. The shoes are hiding in a water drop. The shoes are the stool that a toad sits on. And now a bee. And now a butterfly. And now forever sky.

It's not that the shoes are everywhere. It's that they take me everywhere. It's that I want to go with them, and they make me feel as if I can.

"What are you thinking you're going to find," Hawk interrupts my thoughts, "with your snoops?"

"I don't know," I say. "That's why I'm snooping."

"You think they're just lying around? Clues for the clue collector?"

"Hoping so."

"And what if they're not?"

"The plan is still the plan."

It's getting late. Mom'll call dinner at six and the sun will go down at half past seven. Waiting is hard. I feel the fist of my heart, the stretch of time, the shallow breaths in my shallow lungs, and now I hear Hawk above me, pushing himself forward on the branch. The leaves on the *Hispaniola* rustle.

"Well, hello, there, Mister," Hawk says.

Hawk pushes the Spyglass at me; I don't even have to grab for it. "Look."

I do. I see. It's The Mister tapping away from his lighthouse with his crooked walking stick, the door of the lighthouse shut tight. His white hair puffs, cotton-cloud-like. He heads in the direction of Mountain Dale, which is the direction of the pigs, which is where Dad, in all likelihood, still is. Hawk'll have to be quick. The *Hispaniola* tilts and heaves. Hawk jumps to the ground. Special delivery under his arm. Whistle at his neck. Little brother courage.

My body prickles with the heat, the anticipation. I bury *Book One* in the hollow of the *Hispaniola*. I watch through the Spyglass pressed to my glasses—dial back in on The Mister, who walks too slow for a guy who rides a unicycle in his house at night.

I can hear Hawk running down the hill. Now I don't. Now I see him by the pond, his mop of hair bumping up and down on his head. He cuts left through the fields toward the lighthouse, scattering a gang of peahens and scaring off a fox that runs in its hunch-backed way in one direction, before the peahens scare it back the other way. Hawk is growing cautious now, and he's slowing down to catch his breath. He's walking on the tiptoe part of his boots into the soft dust of the road, and The Mister hasn't turned, it seems The Mister hasn't heard him yet.

Stealth operation. Step by step.

Hawk's practically beside the man before The Mister turns. Just a quick turn, a half peek, and then he turns back, keeps walking in the same direction, toward Mountain Dale, pretending, I would guess, that Hawk is not right there, full of hot-day heat and equipped with a special delivery. Ignoring Hawk is The Mister's plan, that's growing clear enough. But being ignored isn't Hawk's.

Hawk walks beside The Mister steady. Slow as The Mister goes, Hawk goes. All the way down the dusty road until, at last, it's my turn.

The one big chance for the clue collector.

All I Want to Know but Don't

Past the pond, across the field, I follow the hunched fox. Hawk and The Mister are farther down and farther down the road, their backs to me. Mom and Dad are nowhere close. I hurry carefully.

Reach the lighthouse.

Fit my hand onto the brass knob that Dad borrowed from the back door to Old Moe's barn. The door is locked like I knew it'd be, but I had to try, so I did.

There's no key on the hook by the door. No peephole for staring through. No windows until you are three floors up. I head around to the side, to where the chair is folded up and the circle of burned stones and ashes still smells like smoke, and where the crisscross of rope runs from the yard tree and back to the house, empty now, and where the grass is the color of saw-dust.

Nothing.

Useless.

I've still got time.

I circle the lighthouse round to the dusty road, the locked front door, the parked whale of the Cadillac limo. I take a slow, studying walk around, catching snapshots of myself in the shadow-colored limo glass— my long face, my big eyes, the square, black frames of my glasses, my dark hair, which could use a drought-free sudsing.

Once I stop seeing me, I see into the heart of the car. Leather steering wheel. White dials. Black knobs. Long, white stitches on the black seat seams, a couple of watercolor brushes dropped to the floor, a jar of something dark, might be a jar of ink, on the dash-board, a ring of old-fashioned keys hanging from the rearview—other-century keys with rusty teeth.

I don't see much that could count as clues until my third time around, when I look to the backseat of the car, where, spun to a stop, is the rubber wheel of the unicycle and the cushion of the thing. Next to that, stuffed in on its side, is a fat suitcase all bound up by a brown leather strap and silver buckle, and sprinkled in the spaces in between are more jars of ink, a bundle of brushes, a pair of suspenders, one very tiny bright red shoe, and a book or a couple of books about shoes, and books about other things like landscapes and oceans and clouds. There's an old Polaroid camera, like the kind they sell at the county fair. A stash of *Farmers' Almanac*s. A ledger. One mixing bowl. One mixing spoon. A tin can of beans.

But the biggest thing, taking nearly half the seat, is a crate like the one Ilke Vanderveer'd dropped off, almost fell off her shoes dropping that thing off, but this isn't Ilke's crate. It's a different color and a different shape, and it's thick with paper, so much paper that it doesn't all fit. The paper's spilled to the side. It's dropped to the floor—and most of the pages seem blank, but some of them aren't. Some of them are doodled up with what looks (to me) like dreams. There's pencil in some places and color in others, color that smears or has been brushed away, then drawn, but drawn different. Again.

Some of the paper is folded and unfolded, some of it is wrinkled, then unwrinkled, some of it is x-ed over and crossed out and I know what this is, I know without a doubt: this is the start of *Roundabouts: Book Three*.

The missing book.

The story that half a million kids are waiting for—

and now I see, pressing my face against the window-pane, the jewel eyes of Jolly, and the curl tails of the pigs and the dust hooves of the cows, and the skirts on trees, and the house where I live that was once an old barn and the hay shed that was a hay shed.

I can see us in The Mister's touch.

Roundabouts: Book Three.

What the world wants.

What Ilke's come for.

What isn't finished.

What I've found.

I feel my glasses smoosh to the high part of my nose. I feel my heart beating hard through the fist of the messed-up valve.

I feel crazy.

I feel mishmash.

I feel like hoping and I feel like being sad.

I feel like here, past the glass, is a whole beautiful thing, an ending that feels like a beginning.

But The Mister's packed.

The Mister's leaving.

I hear Hawk's whistle blow.

I jiggle the limo door with my hand, and the door is locked. I jiggle the next door, then walk around to the other side and try each door and walk around again, and there's another warning blow from Hawk's brass whistle.

"I need more time, Hawk," I say to myself, only a whisper. I need more time. I look up at the road and see a doubling blur.

My brother with that special delivery in his hand.

The Mister with two legs and a stick.

If I leave right now, I will be seen.

If I stay, there could be trouble.

If I leave . . .

The Operation Is at Risk

Putting the whole operation at risk," Hawk says. Back in the tree, both of us breathless.

He'd dropped the envelope to make a distraction to buy me time. He'd stopped on the road and The Mister had stopped. He'd blown the whistle again and then another time, not the smartest thing, he says, made him out to be a bumpkin, he says, but what were his choices? I had messed with my own plan. I had not left in time. Hawk blew the whistle, he picked up the envelope, he dusted the dust, and he stood, kept on walking down the road, The Mister beside him, walking as slow as he could, trying to talk to the man.

"And—" I say, practically falling out of the tree. "And? What did The Mister say?"

"Nothing," Hawk says. "The Mister said nothing. He looked at me like he was sad. Worse than sad. Disappointed."

"In you?"

"Probably."

"But you weren't going for Ilke's reward. You were just on a distraction mission."

"What's he supposed to guess?" Hawk says.

"Nothing," I say. "He shouldn't have to."

I knew what happened next, 'cause I was there. I was, by then, hiding behind that Silver Whale, putting the whole operation at risk. The Mister dug out his keys to the lighthouse door. He opened that door. He shut it hard behind him and turned the lock, leaving the special delivery with Hawk, leaving Hawk undone and breathless.

Hawk had played at casual after that, walking away slow, pretending there was nothing to it, just an August meander, a regular letter, no pressure here, just thought he'd ask, have a pleasant evening. Leaving me in my tall crouch on the hiding side of the Silver Whale. Hawk was not doubling back, not looking over his shoulder. He was walking away like he had no care in the world, and all that time I was thinking about Jolly and the cows and our house that used to be a barn and all the parts of *Book Three* in the Cadillac.

When it was probably all clear, I stood up and started walking. When I got to the pond, I walked faster than that. When I got to the hill, I was half running, but not really running, and Hawk was on the path to the tree, forcing a cloud of dust behind him. He was already high in the branches.

I had dust on my glasses now, in my hair, and on my tongue. Hawk was on the branch above me.

"I'm sorry, Hawk," I say now. Mean it.

"I blew the whistle," he says. "Three times, I blew it. He could have seen you, Sara, maybe he did. Blowing the whistle was your plan."

"I was onto something."

"It was a close call."

"Hawk—"

"You could have ruined everything. I trusted you." His voice is so mad and so accusing and I know he's right, but he has to listen.

"But I didn't, Hawk. I didn't blow it. Will you calm down and listen? Don't you want to know what I saw?"

Hawk pushes the leaves between us to one side. He stares down at me. He waits.

"'Course I do."

"He's leaving, Hawk. Looks like he is, anyway."

Hawk's eyebrows shoot up over his two moon eyes. His face is still all red with being mad. "What are you talking about? Leaving?"

"He's packed up. The Silver Whale is stuffed. He's got that crazy bike of his inside. A suitcase. A bunch of books. A pair of suspenders."

"Leaving?" Hawk says, his voice practically hitting a screech. "Leaving?" He jumps down from the tree. He starts walking a circle. He looks up at me. "But he can't leave," he says, like it'll be my fault if that happens. "We can't let him."

"Hawk," I say, looking down at his head.

"What?" He stops.

"There's something else."

"There can't be something else."

"There is." I wrangle down. It takes me a second. I stand looking down at Hawk. He stands looking up.

"There's a crate. A different crate than the one Ilke brought. A not-busted crate. That crate is filled to spill with drawings. The Roundabouts, I figure. *Book Three*."

"No. Way," Hawk says.

"Yeah," I say. "I saw it. It's beautiful, Hawk. It's really beautiful. Sketches, mostly, of right here. Pictures of our farm and the pigs and the sunflowers and Jolly. It's hard to see, but it's easy to tell. The Roundabouts, Hawk. Our farm as inspiration."

Hawk watches me. He puts both arms out, like he needs balance. He won't believe me, but he does. "You sure?"

"Right in the back. Stashed. It's so so so so beautiful, Hawk. But The Mister's leaving."

"Leaving," Hawk says.

"And if he gets away, nobody will know where he is. If he leaves, he'll never finish the thing he came here to do. He needs this farm. He needs our farm, Hawk, us, and Ilke—she's scaring him away. We're scaring him too, with that stupid special delivery. We should have left him straight alone, like Mom said."

"A modern classic," Hawk says, his voice gone straight from anger to awe. "Made right here. On this farm."

"Or maybe would have been. Or maybe it's too late. Maybe we'll never know the end of his story. Maybe he'll never make it."

"What do you think he burned in that bonfire?" Hawk asks, scratching his head and closing his eyes so that he can see the smoke again in his memory.

"No way of knowing."

We turn, look over the trees, past the pond, toward the field, toward the lighthouse. We turn, and I wonder if The Mister can see us.

"What did he say, Hawk, when he saw you with the letter? Bright Star right there, on the envelope. What did you tell him?"

"I just said it'd come direct to our front door, a special delivery," Hawk says. "He took one look and turned away. He wanted nothing of it."

"Did he mention Ilke?"

"No."

"Did he say anything? Think."

"What he said was . . . What he said was 'The vision is mine, nobody else's.'"

"The vision is his."

"That was it. He wasn't happy, I can tell you that. I would say that it was worse than that. I would say he was disappointed."

"In you?"

He shrugs.

"In us?"

"Probably."

"But he needs us, Hawk. Don't you think? He does." I put my hand on my heart to stop its hard beating. I try to catch my breath, but I'm having trouble.

"We can't let him leave."

"How do we stop him?"

"I don't know. Can't figure it."

Leave The Mister alone, Mom said, and we can't ask Mom. We can't ask Dad. We shouldn't be asking Mrs. Kalin.

The sky has turned a blue darker than blue. I clean my glasses with the hem of my T-shirt and put them back on, and I see that the actual color of the actual sky is not sunny-day clear. A storm could be coming. A real one. "Maybe we should tell Mom and

Dad," I say, contradicting my own thinking, going back and forth with my thoughts. "Tell them what happened."

"And say what?" Hawk says. "That M. B. Banks is packing up to leave, and maybe that's because of us, maybe we did some interfering?"

I'm leaning against the tree. He's sitting, knees to his chin, on the ground. He's burying his face in his knees.

"Maybe we should tell them," I say. "Maybe we should tell them what we know, what we were thinking."

"Don't you think they have enough worries?"

"Yeah," I say. "Still."

"Yeah," he says. And he's so completely sad and I feel so completely bad and I don't know what I was thinking. What kind of plan did I have, anyway? Where did I think this would be going?

The sky changes more colors. There are more and more clouds and they're coming faster in. Feels like ginger-ale bubbles against my skin.

"It's going to rain, Hawk," I say. "For real it is. You see it?"

"I see it."

"We've got to get back."

"I know it," Hawk says, but he doesn't stand.

"Hawk?"

"You don't have a next step," he says. "In your plan. Do you?"

"We'll figure it out, Hawk," I say, and throw my arm across his shoulder. "He hasn't left yet. Right? He's still right there, in the lighthouse."

"You really think it'll rain?" Hawk asks, like he hasn't studied all the clouds and their meanings with Mom. Like that hasn't been part of our homeschooling lessons, part of our lives, since the first.

"I think it will rain."

"I thought the skies had forgotten how."

"I don't think the skies think," I say.

"Wish I didn't have to think," he says.

I grab *Book One* from the hollow of the tree. Hawk hugs his special delivery tight against his chest.

Sweet, Soft Thud

We hurry up to our rooms and back down—almost late for dinner. We put out the forks and knives, fold the paper towel napkins. Hawk cracks another frozen log of lemonade concentrate into the pitcher with the leftover orange slices and stirs. Mom steps in through the back door and heads straight past, to the front of the house, and out onto the porch. She goes no farther than that.

"Kids?" she calls. "Kids? You won't guess what." Sticking her head back into the house and calling up to our rooms, to where she thinks we've been, fast asleep and dreaming.

Now Dad is hurrying in through the back door, leaving a basket of eggs on the table and two jars of goat milk, sealed tight against the cats that follow him in. Mom's on her porch rocker by the time Hawk and I step out to join her. When Dad sits down on his own broken bit of wicker, Figgis jumps to his lap and arches her back.

"Front row seats," Dad says. "On our August storm." Not taking his eyes from the sky as Hawk and I settle in. Not looking for us to report on our sleeping afternoon off from our chores. Just looking for hope for his cistern.

"Just let it be," Mom says. "Just let it come."

Closing her eyes as she says it.

It's still just clouds and a more forceful breeze, the atmosphere feeling trapped inside a jar. A thickening. Best show on earth, this will be, this rain that's coming, that will crack the sky, that will turn brown to green and dirt to mud and the dry patch under the bridge to a creek and the cistern into a better place. There are buckets and tubs and Hawk's cannikins and gallipots and one of us will remember them soon—set them down out here so we can catch the stuff, save it, drink it fresh from the clouds—but not just yet.

The first drop of rain is a sweet, soft thud.

The first crack is a light show and a drumroll.

Verdi the rooster puts some opera to it.

"Will you look at that," Dad says.

A Good Night for Candlesticks

*I*t comes for real.

We're wild with forgetting everything we do not have.

We're just us.

No beginnings, no ends, no troubles, and we don't need to hear the stories Mom and Dad won't tell about their afternoon of asking, and they don't need to hear about the mess I think I made, because it's raining and the rain just is, the rain is the moment that we're living in.

We're dancing in the slap and the streak of it. We're plunking rain-catch things down on the lawn, in the garden, by the goats, with the pigs, on the roof. Milk cartons and milking pails. Old pitchers. The plugged-up kitchen sink that's been sitting in the barn. The red wagon and the copper-bottomed pans and the scrub buckets and the coin jars and the flowerpots, every last place where falling water can be safe, plus the three blue barrels where we will pour all the collected stuff whenever the rain doesn't rain anymore.

It's been so long since it rained like this that we have to remember it quick—where we stashed the catching things and where they make the best catching fit: at the bottom of a drain spout, on the bench beside the pond, beneath the shallow stone birdbath, which gets overflowed in minutes—and the more we do, the wetter we are, and the darker it gets, and the cows push their heads out of their barn to catch the kerplunks, and Jolly and Molly and Jo and Polly ring the bells on their necks, and the cats don't know what to do with themselves, and the guinea fowl go very quiet, and Old Moe is full of warthog sounds. Phooey's holed up in the cab of Dad's truck. We'll get a good blue egg out of the excitement.

"Well that's certainly enough," Mom says, when she sees Dad dragging out a plastic duffel bag.

"You're a spoilsport, Becca Weust," Dad says, leaving the duffel inside. He calls Mom her birth-right name whenever he's most in love with her.

"The perennial kid, John," Mom says. "Always a kid."

He takes her in his arms like he's about to do a boardwalk dance. He bends down to give her a kiss.

"Ewww," Hawk says. Mom laughs.

The rain falls like coins from the sky.

I'd forgotten how it sounds, to hear Mom laugh.

We run or almost run. They run. To the barns and back. To the pigs and west. To the pond and to the bridge, hoping for a creek. Hearing the patter as we work. Watching the lightning strike. Seeing the Scholls blinking on and off.

I don't know how long it takes before we're finally all back inside. The floors skidding. The kitchen ransacked, the cats shaking their coats in two separate corners, licking the rain from their fur, our own hands cleaner than they've been. I'm sitting on the inside steps full of dark, sweet drip when the power on the farm goes out. A buzz, a pop, and it fizzles. The hum of every inside motor stops. Time stops. The absolute dark.

"Honey?" Dad calls from somewhere.

"It blew," Mom calls back.

"A good night for candlesticks," Dad says. I hear him scurrying around in that back bedroom of theirs, and now here he is, his chin lit up, a thick flame in his hand. He looks like Christmas Eve when we sing "Silent Night" and pass each other hope, wick to wick.

He has an extra candle and a dish for me, and Hawk's right behind him, lit up too, his hair a dark mop on his head with a halo fringe. Hawk carries a second flame for Mom.

"It was the best of times," Dad says, leaving out the other half of that saying and looking like Dad from a few years ago, a spark in his cheeks and his eyes. The Dad before his daughter got sick. The Dad before the machines began to die. The Dad the banks respected.

"Nobody predicted this," I hear Mom say. "All this rain. Coming from where?"

"Don't kick a gift horse," Dad says, and now Mom's standing here, at the base of the stairs, looking like the sun the way the candle catches her face. There's gold in her eyes and glow in her hair. I think of The Mister in his lighthouse, come all the way here from I still don't know where, parking his Silver Whale and tucking in behind a lavender-wreath door and choosing three round rooms with a few round things. The Mister choosing this farm. Drawing this farm into the pages of his story, his very modern classic in the making. I think of him out ducking in and out of the shadows behind me, into the skirts of evergreens, into the shadows of the goat barn. I think of him not taking Hawk's special delivery, saying only six words, but what do they mean? Every shoot of lightning cracks the darkness of this house, and that means it cracks the lighthouse, too, strikes through the band of upstairs glass, then bumps down quick, spiral step by step.

His things in that car. Himself in that lighthouse, which isn't really a lighthouse. It's just a silo we turned around.

Everything turns around.

Maybe?

Sometimes?

"Pretty sure there's only one choice for dinner," Mom says. She leads the way into the kitchen with one hand cupped around her yellow flame. I hear her put the dishes out where we'd already laid the forks and knives, the paper towel napkins. I hear her open and close the refrigerator door, quick, to keep the chill in. We fumble our way to our seats as the cutting begins. A slice of Strawberry Wonder pie for each one of us. Seconds, soon enough. A nice fresh smell where there'd been smoke.

Who knows what time it is? It doesn't matter. Who cares that both cats have jumped up onto the table and are licking our four plates clean now that the second servings are done? Who really wants tomorrow to come? Who needs the lights, when we are the light?

Good as good gets. Don't look ahead and don't look back, and that's the truth of it, and that's what The Mister sees. That's what The Mister sees when he looks at us. Or. That is what he drew.

The rain is talk. The rain explains itself. The rain doesn't lie, and it does not tell the truth. The rain does not have to ask. Our candles are burning to their little stubs. Our clothes are cardboard crunch. The floor's so wet that our candlelight makes it look like an ice-pond slick. The cats have strawberry tongues.

"The day is drawing its curtains closed," Dad finally says, and I don't know if that's an original or something hanging on the wall.

"Time," Mom says, "for bed."

"Appreciate," Hawk says, "how you gave us the afternoon off."

"Appreciate," I say. Enough.

One by one we push back our chairs and stand. We leave the plates where they are, to the cats.

"Good night," we say. "Good night. Good night." Hawk and me on the stairs now, and heading up. Mom and Dad tracing around, to their room. I find my door by candlelight. I turn the knob. I stop.

"Twenty minutes," Hawk whispers. "My room."

"Twenty minutes," I say, a more or less guess, since no one has a working clock. I close the door behind me, candlelight my way to the windows, slammed shut. I stand there watching the dark and the dying lightning strikes through the blur of the rain. I listen to the big kerplunks of water falling, filling, still.

More on What We Know So Far

Hawk sits on his bedroom floor with his candle blown out, his flashlight spilling light. I sit close, wearing dry pants, a dry shirt, dry rain-cleaned hair at last. We smell like rain. Rain's a good, clean smell.

"What are we going to do?" Hawk wants to know. "About The Mister?"

"Thinking," I say.

He pages through *Roundabouts: Book Two*, looking for his own clues. He shoves the book in my direction so I can see what he sees. There are cities built of mushroom caps. There are countries inside nests. The red shoes are huge beside snowflakes and small beside giraffes and full of splash in summer creeks. They're walking up the bark of trees, the green of stalks, the shine of seeds, and you wouldn't think that there's story in it, but it's story, true. It's like the shoes are you or the shoes are me, the shoes are how we dream.

Every page, and there's more beauty in it.

"What does it mean?" Hawk asks, closing the book, leaning his head against the bed. "About The Mister? What does it say?"

"That he sees what isn't," I say.

"Yeah," Hawk says, scratching his head.

"I think it's a story about aloneness," I say, lying on my side now, paging through the book again. "I mean: there's only this one pair of shoes."

"Aloneness," Hawk says. "Or differentness."

"Why not both?" I say, pulling the knots from my hair.

"See how it ends?" Hawk says, taking the book from me. He turns to the last picture, which spills across two pages. "It ends here," he says, pointing to the pair of shoes on an ice-snow cliff. "Right here. See how it is? There's a blue river below. There's a world across. Shoes could only get to the next place by taking a running leap."

Hawk slides the book from his lap to mine. He throws the cone of light onto the scene. I sit up to study it. Hawk waits.

"You see it?" he says.

"I see it," I say.

A cliff of snow. A split of earth. A field of green. Looks like a farm to me, that green. Looks like people on that farm. Looks like the shoes could have some people company. If the shoes take the running start. If they leap.

Hawk lets the flashlight light beam straight up. It catches floating dust in its yellow stream.

"You see any people in *Book One*?" he asks.

"No."

"You see any people in *Book Two*?"

"Not except for this page," I say.

"These red shoes have gone all over everywhere, and now they're standing on the edge." Hawk points again at the last picture. "Last page of *Book Two*, and the shoes have to choose."

"Come on."

"What else?"

Hawk shifts the light. He hardly breathes. I take my time, one finest detail, then the next. The stretch of green, the fields of hay, the tractor chugging—I can hardly see it, but it's there. The pond, the herd of cows, the peahens—barely the width of a pen tip, not even half the height of a short fingernail. The coop of chickens and a hand collecting eggs—I'm sure that's what it is. The barn where the goats live and the barn where the people live and the curl of smoke coming from the chimney. The silver silo in the distance.

"It's like he was here before he even moved in," I say. "Like he had this place in mind."

"He's hiding," Hawk says. "Wouldn't you? From Ilke?"

"Watch this," he says, and he turns. He reaches for something underneath his bed and hands it to me.

"Take a look," he says.

It's the special delivery envelope with the Saran pulled off. It's the special delivery envelope with a slit. One major rule in the House of Scholl is that nobody ever butts into anybody's stuff. Private is private. Those are the rules, even if you're not family. Even if you're Ilke Vanderveer, with the crazy shoes and the big Rover that drove all the way down here from Manhattan.

"You're going to be in so much—" I tell Hawk.

"Just look," he says.

I look.

Dear Martin:

I've talked to the publisher. He agrees. If we are to
succeed with *Roundabouts: Book Three*—if we are to give
readers the Big Ending that we think our readers need—the
shoes will have to disappear. The shoes will have to vanish.

We need the drama, Martin.

We need crescendo.

We need the really big.

We need you to agree.

We've returned your sketches, with my markups. We've
created sample spreads of our own—just some sketches,
Martin, just some hints of the direction we'd like the story to
go. We've sent you reams and reams and reams of paper, so
that there'll be no excuses, Martin.

No more excuses, Martin.

We can't miss another publishing season.

We cannot, quite simply, miss.

If you have questions, you know where I am. Josie's on
call if you need her.

I require a reply.

—Ilke

Whose Story Is a Story?

So," I say, after I've read the words twice, after I've thought about them. "Ilke has her own version of The Mister's story."

"But shouldn't he be able to—"

"Seems to me he should—"

"Shouldn't everyone be able to—"

"I think so. Yeah. I do."

I stare out into the night. Try to see the lighthouse from where I am. It's hard.

"So he comes here—"

"To hide," Hawk says. He stands up too. He stands

beside me. He can see what I can't see. He can figure what I'm thinking.

"He comes here and the farm is something he loves so much that he starts to draw it. He wants his shoes to take the running leap. He wants—"

"Less aloneness," Hawk says. "Less differentness."

"We think," I say. "Anyway."

Hawk leans his head against my shoulder like he used to do when we were small, when nobody knew about Marfan, when it was just two kids on a farm, the worries of a farm, and not the extra worries about the facts of me that were still hidden. We hear the spluttering rain through the dark of the night. I watch the window for The Mister. "We've got to tell her what we think," Hawk spurts out. "We've got to tell her that The Mister's shiny shoes need to be The Mister's shiny shoes."

"Those red shoes are not disappearing," I say. "They can't. They won't." I say the words through a choke in my throat.

Hawk starts pacing. Back and forth. "But if we tell her what we know, she'll know we opened up her letter."

"She shouldn't have given you that letter," I say. "Anyway."

Hawk stops pacing. His flashlight beam points to the

floor, then bounces up and there we are, in the window glass, looking back at one another.

"But now we know," I say. "And now that we know, we have to do something. Mom and Dad would want us to. Do the right thing, that's what they'd say."

"But Mom and Dad," Hawk says, "don't know. Mom and Dad can't."

"So it's up to us," I say.

Hawk's silent.

"The Mister needs time to make the story he wants," I say.

"You can't buy time," Hawk says. "If you could, we'd have already done it."

I think of Dad at the bank. I think of Mom with her pies. I think of Mom and Dad with their friends and Mom with her talk of selling everything we have so that we can buy what we need for the surgery in Cleveland, the David procedure, which I don't understand, but I do understand that it would buy me more time. Time, time, time. That's the thing. For us, and for The Mister.

I crouch back down to the floor. Hawk crouches too, turns the flashlight off. I think of all the pictures of The Mister that I have in my head. The Mister holding Phooey. The Mister's shadow after mine. The Mister's hand in the crisscross of his lines, his hands on the pages, his ideas, his burning smoke.

"We need to talk to Ilke," I tell Hawk.

"Talk to her?"

"Explain some things but not explain others."

In the dark beside me, Hawk thinks. It's like I can hear his brain on a whirl.

"We could call her," he says, throwing his legs out in front of him. "We have her number."

"I'm not talking about calling her, Hawk. I'm talking about an in-person face-to-face. I'm talking heart-to-heart persuasion."

I feel Hawk turn toward me in the dark. His eyes on the me he can't see. His jaw in a drop.

"Nothing's impossible," I say. "According to you."

"You betting on her coming back?" he says, a whisper, like all of a sudden he's worried about Mom listening in, or Dad.

"I'm betting on us going for a visit."

"She works in New York City, Sara. New York City."

"I know."

"You ever been to New York City?"

"Have you?"

"You thinking of driving my tractor? Of asking Isaiah for a Spots express? Of stealing Dad's truck for the day?"

"Nope."

"What, then?"

"Let me think," I say. I think. "I'm working," I say, "on a plan."

"Well," he says.

"Face-to-face," I say. "It's the only way."

Outside the rain drips.

The rain drips.

The rain drips.

"We're going to New York City," Hawk says.

"Yeah," I say. "We are."

Hope Is the Plan

The only sound anywhere is rain. The gulp and the gush and the slurp and the plunk. The wash and the rinse on the windowpanes, the knocking, like someone's walking, on the roof, and my mind whirls, it whirls, it whirls.

I am twelve and Hawk is eleven, and this is us, this is now. I am me and he is he and this is our summer, drought season, a burned-down shed and hay that's missing and banks that will not listen, and The Mister, and the only future is the future you make, and everybody, all the time, is choosing.

We're going to New York City.

Even if the banks won't talk to Dad. Even if there isn't enough fruit, not enough sugar, not enough crust, not enough people in this whole town or the next three towns for four thousand of Mom's pies. Even if we can't cash in on the mysterious reward for the mysterious package that The Mister will not take. Even if. So long as The Mister is here, so long as he stays, so long as he stays, hope is the plan.

I feel a rumble in the floor, a little shake. The house turns on, the power is back, the yellow juice of electricity flows into lightbulbs, refrigerator, clocks. The dryer beeps like it does when it's been out of whack.

Dawn.

Up the hill, Dad'll be visiting the cistern. In the goat shed the goats bray, and now, standing at the window, my glasses on, I see the lighthouse blink. I can barely make out the Silver Whale, sitting in the narrow road of mud. I can barely see the red front door, hardly get a glimpse of the round room beyond the third-floor glass. But there is something moving. Something there.

Someone. Restless. Waiting.

"Hello, Mister." I wave.

"Don't leave," I say, my words fogging up my own window glass.

Don't leave yet.

Full Report

Dad gives us the first report, all of us standing there, in the kitchen—Mom in her pajamas and flip-flops, Hawk in his yellow shirt and jeans, me in a better shirt than the one I've been wearing and a pair of denim shorts.

The pond is as good as a lake, Dad says. The algae has skimmed off to one side, been beaten back by the fallen rain. The ducks are going wild. The lost creek beneath the wooden bridge has shown up again, size of a snake, Dad says, a big one. The pigs are in a full mud roll and the coats of the goats are all matted down from the rain dance they must have done. The cows are licking the rain off the bark of the trees and off the chains by the fence and the birds are so full of talk Dad says he said to tone it down, but the birds didn't listen, they're still going at it, full of the scratch and squawk of their songs.

"Walked the hill," Dad says, "because the roads are so mud thick, the truck tires did nothing but spin." Walked the hill at dawn, Dad says, and got up to the cistern quick, and the cistern water is a good eight inches higher than it's been, that's his biggest news, and it'll get higher still once Mom and Hawk and he finish the big pour—gather all the rainwater in all the pails and the barrels and the buckets and the bowls and get it up the hill in wheelbarrows and the truck when the road is dry. They'll fill that cistern with every delicious inch.

"The rain has done its work," Dad says, and Mom smiles, and when she smiles, Hawk smiles, and now I smile, and we're all pretty goofy with it, forgetting, for this minute, the things on the farm that are waiting on us, the goats, for one thing, the ripe stuff that needs a good pick, the warm eggs, Phooey's egg, wherever she went and put it, the money we still don't have, and Dad hasn't even started breakfast yet and it looks like he might not, like he's taking the day off from flapjacks, and nobody cares, nobody asks, nobody talks about anything except for the rain.

"I'm making waffles," I say. Dad yanks out his beat-up kitchen chair and sits. Mom follows, and Hawk, and all eyes are on me. I open drawers, I open the fridge, I grab what I need: the flour, the milk, the sugar, yesterday's eggs, the baking powder, the salt, Mom's best vanilla. The glass bowl and the mixing spoon, the waffle pan.

"Better be good," Hawk says.

"They will be," I say.

Touch Back

Where the mud dries on our skin, we crease. Where it's still wet and new, we're slick. We're out with the animals and the earth and the buckets and the pails doing our chores, and the hours go on, and the sun is coming in. Bright sun in a clean sky. The rear ends of white clouds mirrored back from the face of the pond, in the snake of the creek, in the fat water drops that don't quite fall from leaves.

Now Mom's downstairs making fresh potato pie and outside, on the roof, Hawk is standing at my window, knocking against the middle pane.

I put *Roundabouts: Book One* down and roll off

the bed—but I'm still following the pair of red shoes around and through and sometimes up in my head. Sometimes, on the winter pages, you don't see the shoes; you see just the prints they leave behind. Sometimes, in the summer, the shoes are very hard to find, tucked into the dark patches of shade. Sometimes, in the autumn, there's only the smallest tip of one shining shoe poking out from a pile of leaves, and on a blue-black sea, there is a big fat whale with those red shoes like a hat on its watery head.

Everywhere the red shoes go, the red shoes are. Everywhere they go, I am. That is the magic I can't understand: how all this pretty and odd and wild and bright can come from a solitary man. The beauty and the sad of it. The bold and the shy. The funny and the quiet. Everything in the Roundabouts The Mister must have felt or must have seen, somewhere or somehow, even if only in his head.

What has he felt here?

What has he seen here?

What was he looking for when he was following me?

What does he still need to find?

The Mister can't leave until he finds his whole story.

The Mister can't leave until he chooses his own story.

There's half a million readers waiting.

There's Hawk.

And now there's me. And he can't leave with his ending until I know mine, a thought I think, and then I try to unthink it.

Hawk knuckles the window, impatient. "Come on!" He makes a face and leaves. I climb out toward him, past the buckets of rain that we'll bring to Dad in a while.

"Saved by the rain," Hawk says, kicking his feet out over the edge and helping me down. He hands me his Spyglass so I can see what he means. "Saved by the rain and the mud."

"You're not kidding," I say. The Mister's out there behind the wheel of his whale, his tires spitting mud, a crazy spin. The Mister takes his foot off the accelerator. He leaves the engine on, gets out. He walks to the back end of the whale, his shoulders going up and down with his limp. He puts his weight against it, shoves.

Doesn't budge an inch, and why would it budge an inch? It rained buckets. The earth is mud.

"Only way he could get that limo out of here is if we help him," Hawk says, taking his Spyglass back.

I give him a look.

"That's not the plan," I remind him.

"Still hazy on the plan," Hawk says. He looks at me. Full-on looks at me. His big moon eyes in his pale face, a couple of new summer freckles on his nose. He's depending on me to figure this out. I'm planning on figuring it out.

"We need the phone and Mom and Dad out of listening range."

"Easy," Hawk says. "Consider it done."

"We need fifty, sixty dollars."

"Not so easy."

"We need a hanger."

"A hanger?"

"Wire hanger. You know. And we need Isaiah and Spots. First thing tomorrow. Down at the end of the road. Ready to roll."

Hawk shakes his head. "Spots isn't trotting from here to Manhattan, Sara."

"That would be a known fact."

"So?"

"What?"

Hawk looks at me funny, changes his question: "So what time do you want the two of them here?"

"Sunrise. A little before, would be best."

"This afternoon," Hawk says, "I'll find Isaiah, tell him we're drawing on favors again. Sure as I know him, he'll come."

"We'll get him something from the city."

Hawk blinks.

"You know. Something for thanks."

"Don't need to do that."

"It'd be a nice touch."

"Focus on the plan, Sara. Focus on the plan."

I nod. I study the lighthouse. The silver in the sun. The Mister back inside his borrowed three round rooms. Mud on his boots. Tires in a rut.

"That cash," I say, "will be the hardest part."

"Got me a notion," Hawk says, a smile spreading across his face, a blush in his cheeks. "Just occurring. Just coming in." He touches his head with his finger. "Bingo," he says.

I hear the peahens in their strut and the ducks on the pond. I hear Verdi tuning up for a big song. I hear Mom downstairs, starting to call for us. Hawk jumps up, to head her off at the pass.

"Rendezvous," he tells me. "Midafternoon. The *Hispaniola*."

He looks over his shoulder and lifts his fist. He touches his knuckles to that part of the low sky. I raise my fist to his hand.

living Is living

*C*hicken Pimiento Potato pie. Mom's best, we all say, ever. She's left the bandanna off her head and her hair falls free, the strands of gray wrapping a few loose curls. She has put some lip gloss on, a little eye shadow. She wears a white shirt with some fake lace that runs around the collar. It's like there are five people at the table and one of them is the special guest called Rain. We gather here in its honor.

Mom cuts the pie into wide slices and serves up seconds. Dad keeps reporting on the farm. Roads still too muddy for the pickup truck, but the tractor working fine. Phooey's eggs in an old squirrel nest that had fallen from a tree. The cows taking their time with the hay, like they had filled themselves up with rainwater.

All through lunch, I'm quiet. All through lunch, I'm thinking, fitting the last few pieces of the puzzle together in my head, playing them out straight and playing them out round, imagining the mess I could make or the good I could find, the trouble I'll start or the hope I can prove.

Red shoes look good on any feet, doesn't matter how long or how stretchy.

Please Be Specific

Hawk is going to buy us time, and by that I mean he's put himself in charge of Mom and Dad, who are outside filling the barrels with the rain that fell last night. He'll keep them busy, he'll help as he does, and I'll stay right here and do my thing. This is the plan that we have.

"How much time will you need?" he asked me.

"Fifteen minutes," I said. "At least."

Now I find Ilke Vanderveer's card in Hawk's room, where he left it, pressed between the pages of *Treasure Island*. I head for Mom and Dad's room, sacred country. The one place on the whole farm that belongs only to them. The door is closed but it's never locked. It creaks on its hinges, and I'm in.

The room is full of blue-sky sun—windows on three sides and a skylight up top, one wall the color of Phooey's best eggs, the rest of it the color of regular shells. There's a chest of drawers and a king-size bed. The bed is neat with its blue covers on. The winter quilt is folded on one end. But it's the old-fashioned ivory-colored phone by their bed that I want, its cord all tangled like it gets. I walk in my socks, as quiet as I can, as if Mom and Dad could hear me from outside.

It's obvious. They can't.

It's now or never.

It's now.

I pick up the phone. Study Ilke Vanderveer's card. Press my hand over my wild, too-big, thumping heart.

One. Two. One. Two. I start, pressing the numbers with the sweaty tip of my index finger. Five. Five. Finishing the number off. Practicing the lines I thought up when I was making the plan. Somebody answers two rings in. A woman with a smart voice who is busy, I can tell.

"Bright Star Publishing," the voice says. Crisp and clipped.

"Hello," I say. I barely say it. It's like all my words have suddenly fallen straight down to my wild, thumping heart.

"Bright Star?" it repeats. Even quicker this time. More curt.

"Yes," I say. "Please." Trying to sound like an adult. "I'd like to speak with Ilke Vanderveer?"

"Your name?"

"Sara Scholl."

"Sara who?"

"Scholl."

"What is the nature of your call?"

The nature? I think. *The nature?*

The voice on the other end starts talking before I can. It rattles off a list of nots, a speech it seems to always give. "If you are calling about a manuscript, we do not accept unagented submissions. If you are calling about rights, I'll connect you to our rights department. If you are calling about our fall list, I'll connect you to publicity."

The voice stops. Waits.

"It's none of that," I say.

"Please be specific."

Outside, I can see Mom and Dad and Hawk filling the last blue barrel with the rain of bowls and pots. I can see the hurry in the operation, how the more they get done, the faster it goes, and how Hawk can't slow it down.

"It's top secret," I blurt out.

"Top secret?" The voice almost laughs. "You think

you've heard everything," it says, "and then you hear this. Top secret." The voice practically shakes its head.

"It concerns M. B. Banks."

"Is that a fact?"

"Yes."

"Do you know how many times a week somebody calls and tells me that?"

"No, ma'am," I say, instantly kicking myself. I say "ma'am" and I'm a kid. I say "ma'am" and I'm a kid straight off a farm. I'm a kid, and my phone cover is shot, this receptionist is going to cut me off, this plan I have is falling flat, I need to speak to Ilke.

"You hear one M.B. story and then you hear another," the voice says. "M.B. sightings. M.B. hoaxes. M.B.— We do not currently have a publication date for *Roundabouts: Book Three*," the voice says, interrupting itself, going back to the script, it sounds like a script, a machine talking. "We can put you on our e-mail list, if that would help. We could—"

It's a spiel. Dad likes that word, "spiel." I have no time for a spiel.

I break the spiel. "Ilke Vanderveer met my brother, Hawk," I say, giving up my cover. "She talked to him. She gave him her card. She said to call if—"

"If what?"

"If something came up."

"Is that right," the voice says.

"Something's come up," I say.

"I'll give her a message," the voice offers, after a moment. I can hear people in the background, the ring of other phones, the noise of Bright Star.

"Talking to her would be best."

"You know how many times I've heard that? Ilke Vanderveer's in a meeting. She can't speak with you right now."

Mom is pouring the last bucket of water into the third blue barrel. She's holding the tin above her own head and watching the rainwater spill down, a little waterfall. Done. She kisses Dad on the cheek, she hugs Hawk with both arms, she straightens her lace collar. She's coming.

"Acquisition meeting," the voice says now. "Not available."

"Will she be available tomorrow?"

"Perhaps you should write to her," the voice says. "Do you have our street address?"

"Ilke Vanderveer asked us to call. She gave us her card. Gave it to Hawk, who is my brother. Gave it to him with a special delivery and said there'd be a reward. I have news on the special delivery. We want our reward."

I can hear the voice deciding. I can hear it— suddenly not precisely sure, as if my story might be a true story, as if maybe, just maybe, it's heard of the

Scholls before, of the town in Pennsylvania, where a kid shows up on a dirt road talking about a pig on the run. "She could be," the voice says. "Available tomorrow." As if it almost trusts me, or almost wants to think that I am telling the truth, that Ilke met Hawk, that Ilke told Hawk to call, that whatever has gone wrong with *Roundabouts: Book Three*, is finally about to go right. She's isn't sure. She stalls.

"You could try again tomorrow," she says.

"In the afternoon?" I ask. "Tomorrow?" Making sure, doing it fast, because Mom's really, really coming now, she's definitely on her way. Leaving the back drive, walking around front, a couple of empty buckets in her hand. They're fruit buckets. They live on the front porch. She's headed there to put the buckets back, and I drop to the floor, talk as quietly as I can to Bright Star reception. Under the apple trees, Mom comes. I hear the buckets hit the wood porch floor. I hear her open the door. She's coming in. She's almost here. She'll find me in her room.

"If nothing changes, Ilke will in fact be here tomorrow afternoon," the voice says. "You can call back then."

"Thank you," I say. "Thank you so much." Hurrying the phone back into the cradle. Hurrying away from this room. Hearing Mom's flip-flops flapping and the hinges on the screen door and Mom inside now, calling my name, looking right into the kitchen first, then looking left, and I'm here.

"How'd it go?" I ask.

"Three full barrels," Mom says, her white shirt damp, her eyes still full of sun. "That was one beautiful storm."

"Cistern's going to fill like a swimming pool," I say.

"You know it is." She smiles.

I take a picture of Mom smiling in my mind.

I take a picture, which is like a seed, the way it keeps its beauty folded in.

The way it wants to go on forever.

Tell Me When

I hear Hawk before I see him—his Doc Martens splashing the path ahead, his lungs rasping. He climbed the hill fast as that kid can climb.

"Got it," he says. Still out of breath. He pulls the hanger from under his shirt and holds it high. The metal catches a piece of the sun. The tree leaves rustle.

"Got this, too," he says. Pulling his wallet out now, which is fat full of cash. He stands straight, still breathing hard, his Spyglass dangling, his brass whistle. He thumbs through the bills, a grin on his face. He reaches through the leaves, hands me the wallet, and more rain falls. It's the heaviest wallet I've ever seen—mostly one-dollar bills and a couple of fives, every bill looking like it'd been wadded up and tossed into the trash and smoothed out crinkled-flat again.

"Hawk," I say, taking my whole brother in.

"Yeah," he says.

"How did you—"

"Kind of a long story."

"I mean—"

"I'll tell you. I promise. But not now, Sara, don't make me."

He reaches past me, grabs the branch above my head, and hoists himself up. He sits in his tree seat. I stay on the ground.

"What's next?" he asks.

I want to know how he got the cash. I want to know if Isaiah said yes. I want to know if this plan is going to work. "Next," I say, "is we wait."

"We wait for what?"

"For him, The Mister. We wait for him to take a walk."

"Not that again."

"That again."

"He in a walking mood?"

"Better be, Hawk. Only way we work the plan is if The Mister walks."

"So The Mister walks," Hawk says. "All right. The Mister walks." As if it is all already in the works. As if my wish is the command. Hawk works the lookout, primo.

"Then what?"

"Then you pop the lock on the Silver Whale."

Hawk whistles. Then he hums. "Pop the lock. With the hanger."

"Pop it." I show him what I mean with my hands.

"Like a regular criminal," Hawk says, with a new whistle. "And as soon as we're in?"

"We collect." I say it like I'm completely sure. I say it like this is the perfect plan.

"What do we collect?" Hawk says quietly. "Precisely?"

"Some of the best of *Roundabouts: Book Three*. Just to borrow. Just to prove. Just to work our persuasion on Ilke."

"It's a risky operation."

"It's what we have."

"We're sure?"

"We're sure. There's half a million readers waiting. There are the shoes themselves. The shoes gotta choose their ending."

"So we wait," Hawk says.

"You watch," I say, looking up into the tree, seeing just his boots, feeling yesterday's rain kerplunk onto my head. "You tell me when."

When

"And . . . we're . . . on," Hawk says.

"Serious?" My heart bumps.

"Taking his constitutional. Look."

Hawk pushes his Spyglass my way. I see. The red door on the lighthouse is cracked. A walking stick pokes. An old man's leg. A second leg. A hat on a head and a head.

"It's him!"

"Of course it's him!"

"We're on!"

It's now or never!

The Mister makes his way to the Silver Whale, opens the door, and hauls himself in. He turns the engine with his key, and the front wheels spin, tossing the mud to the sky and back to the puddles and up on the windshield. The noise scatters a bunch of birds. Birds the size of mosquitoes. I watch the birds for half a second and then I watch The Mister—his head thrown back against the cushion.

Where would he go if that Silver Whale could swim?

What would he think if he could see us here, on the top of the hill, in the *Hispaniola*, waiting for him to walk away, down the road?

Hawk and me, like two Robin Hoods. Straight out of another Scribner.

He's given up. He hauls himself out of the car and slams the door and stands there, and now he's walking, slow slow slow down the road toward the village of pigs, toward Mountain Dale Road, looking for whatever he looks for when he walks, swerving as he goes between the puddles that are full of the glisten of the sun. He could be a turtle the way he moves, his head pushing ahead of the hunch in his shoulders, but he moves, and I catch sight of his shoes and their red polish, their sky and dirt, their speed and stop, their everywhere of anything—those shoes standing on a cliff deciding what they want to choose.

Hawk jumps down and his Doc Martens throw up a soft, muddy splash.

"It's now," I say, and he's off. I watch him run the

path until I can only hear him run. I set off myself, and by the time I'm down the hill and around the pond and across the field, and to the car, The Mister is out of sight, and Hawk has done the hanger trick, popped the lock, opened the door to where the treasure is, sprawled across the seat.

Falling Out of Time

You weren't lying," Hawk says, looking in over the beautiful mess in The Mister's car, which is definitely packed for leaving. "You were straight-up true. This is—"

"I know it," I say.

"Crazy beautiful," Hawk says.

He leans in beside me, past the wheel of the one-wheel bike and strapped-up suitcase and the pair of suspenders. Past me toward the crate, the watercolor spills and ink, the pictures that are half-done or hardly there, sometimes complete. All these places where the red shoes have been, where The Mister has put them, drawn them, thought them. The Mister's seen it, and then he's dreamed it, filling parts of it in with blues and greens and leaving parts of it to brown-gray sketch.

I want to stay all day, look hard and think, but I can't; we have to hurry. We have to choose three or maybe four of these and get out quick, and now I sort while Hawk stands and keeps the lookout, marks the time, makes sure The Mister doesn't catch us here, busting his privacy.

Proof is what Ilke needs. Proof that his version of his story is better than her version of his story. Proof that he has the perfect ending, the best *Book Three*. Our farm is here, more of our farm than there should be. More than he had the chance to paint since he moved in. I know it's true, I feel it.

The bell on the barn, the cracks in the fence, Phooey's eggs in the cab of Dad's truck, the hay dust that falls like miracle snow, and now, shuffling through, leaning in, moving through the strokes and starts of these pictures, I stop and catch my breath. I don't believe and then I do believe what I am seeing—these pictures of Hawk and me. Us. Hawk with his pigs and me with my seeds and Hawk with his tractor and me with Jolly and Hawk and me, in *Roundabouts: Book Three*, the red shoes following us, in the shadows of us, on our roads with us, and beneath our trees with us and now, toward the bottom of the dig, Hawk still keeping watch, I find a picture, half ink, half sketch, of a tall boy and a taller girl side by side at the edge of a pier, a Spyglass lifted high to the boy's eyes, fireflies freckling the skies.

"Hawk," I say. "Jeez. Hawk." So much burn inside of me. So much that hurts my heart.

"You have to hurry."

"You have to see."

"Can't, Sara. Not right now. Go on and make it quick."

I'm quick.

I'm really quick.

We are falling out of time.

"The Mister's coming!" Hawk whispers loud. "You have to make it quick!"

"No kidding," I whisper-shout.

And stand up straight.

And shut the door.

And run, both of us running.

The Morning Will Never Come, It Comes

I hear Hawk washing up. I hear him pulling on his better jeans and buckling his belt, and then he slides back down the hall with his clean socks on and knuckles my door and says, "All yours."

I hurry.

I shower, quick, because it never matters how high the cistern is, there could be another drought tomorrow.

I dress.

It could work, my plan.

It could be the worst disaster.

The pictures we stole are in a soft leather pouch,

except that they're not stolen, they're borrowed. The cash is thick in Hawk's wallet. We've left *Roundabouts: Books One* and *Two*, behind, stuffed beneath our beds, but Hawk's got his Spyglass and his special delivery, and we have our map of New York City thanks to a homeschooling project we did last spring about the cities of our United States, the biggest and most famous. The maps came in the mail, with the rest of the home-school stuff. I found New York tucked up onto the pantry shelf late last night, with the excellent help of Hawk's flashlight.

The last piece of our puzzle.

The Silver Whale is still out there, its wheels dug into the rain-carved ruts. The moon is low in the sky, but there's still no sun. The fireflies sleep and the stars are moving on, and I know this because Hawk says this, because he's standing here, in my room, beside me now, looking out the window past the waves of hay we never put in the shed, the hay that has no home now.

"You ready for this?" Hawk says.

"I'm ready."

En Route

Isaiah's there at the end of our road, just like he said he would be. The sun has cracked the horizon and a splat of yellow runs like a highway stripe from the far hill, across the far field, over Mountain Dale Road in the direction of the Pig Village, putting shine into the wet things, a low glow. Spots flicks the flies with his tail, and Hawk and I are in. Nobody out here, and the day is still cool. Isaiah turns to us and smiles.

"You were right, Hawk," he says.

"Told you so."

"It gets in your head, and sticks," Isaiah says, and I don't know what they're talking about and now, sick feeling in my gut, I do. "It's far away and fiction, but you read it again and it's not. It's—"

"Hawk?" I say, my stomach Ferris-wheeling beneath my heart. Spots clops out in front of us. The breeze reaches us in the back. Hawk won't look at me, he won't turn, he won't answer the question I haven't asked him, I don't need to ask him. *Kind of a long story,* he'd said, up at the tree, meaning the cash, and it occurs to me, just as I'm sitting here, that I saw no *Treasure Island* tepee in Hawk's room late last night when we had our last rendezvous, maybe I saw not one single Scribner Classics classic on his shelves— maybe I didn't because they weren't there, because Hawk has sold his classics for cash, because cash is what we needed, and I asked.

"Did you—?"

Hawk shakes his head, sheepish. And that's all the answer I'll get, that's all the proof he'll give that he has sold his *Red Badge of Courage,* his *Yearling,* his *Last of the Mohicans, Peter Pan,* and *Robin Hood,* his *Treasure Island,* his Blind Pew, his Long John Silver. He gave the classics up, for this.

Oh.

Hawk.

I dig my elbow into his ribs. Dig harder. He won't turn to look at me. He looks straight ahead, like he can't feel me, like I'm not sitting right beside him, asking with the hard point of my long elbow, *Did you really?* Isaiah keeps talking about the start of *Treasure Island*, the bold N. C. Wyeth pictures, the captions that make him want to read fast, and now he wants to know where are we heading to, our final destination, and I don't answer that, I just say, we're headed to the train depot in Lionsberg. There's an 8:05 express.

"Express to where?" Isaiah asks, his face full of sudden interest.

"Express to Philadelphia," I say. Then, don't know why, it isn't necessary, it wasn't part of my plan to announce it: "Then from Philadelphia to New York by way of bus."

"New York?"

"New York City."

Isaiah whistles, a long, low, you-telling-the-truth-on-me-now? sound. Spots's ears pull back. Isaiah hitches us up to a trot, and the world rolls past. The red cows at Charlotte and Jane's. Grencik sheep, all nose to nose. The silver silos and the red barns and the hex signs and the rust. Hawk sold his Scribners, without telling me. His whole entire Scribners. Sold. And I borrowed money from Mom's pie tin, not telling Hawk, even though it is her extra money, her save-it-until-Christmas stash.

Please don't worry, I wrote in the note that I left behind on my bed. *We'll be back. Important business to do, and we're doing it.*

Trust us, I said.

Wondering if they suspect. If they've seen us spying, lying, breaking the rules, but desperate times call for desperate measures, isn't there some quote like that? Something Dad said? Something framed? And wouldn't they do it too, if they knew what we knew, if they'd seen Ilke for themselves, if they'd read the special delivery, if they'd paid close attention, like we've paid attention, to The Mister walking our roads, hiding in our shadows?

Wouldn't they?

Shouldn't we have told them?

We should have told them, but what had Mom said? *Leave The Mister alone.*

And we had promised.

I don't know how they'll ever fix my heart or who will pay for the David or what is going to happen now, because there'll be no fix, no David. I don't know when the banks will forgive Dad's loans or when insurance will forgive the fire or when my body will stop stretching. I don't know when Mom will get to bake her pies on the days she wants to bake her pies, and not on a by-demand schedule. I don't know when the cistern water will rise so high that Dad will finally stop checking.

I don't know most anything, but today, right now, I know this: sometimes when it seems that you're losing it all, you have to quit thinking about how you're losing.

Hurry, Spots, I think. *Hurry, Isaiah, who owns the Scribner Classics now. I'm sorry, Hawk. I'm sorry.*

It's a ten-mile ride to the depot. It's like sitting inside a hiccup in the carriage.

When we reach the light at the top of the long hill, we stop. When the light turns green we start again, down the hill now, around another curve, toward the stub of Main Street. We pass the small brick houses, the tall white church, and now—I lean forward, then quickly back—there's Mrs. Kalin out in her library garden, deadheading flowers, straightening the stakes that hold up the dahlias. She stands up straight just as we go past. She fits one hand above her eyes and stares into the rising sun and thinks that maybe she sees me. She tries to wave us down, but we keep going. She turns now, she hurries from the garden.

"I think she saw us," I say to Hawk.

"Maybe," he says. "Maybe not."

"But what if—"

"Shhhh," he says. "The plan is already in motion. Your plan," he says, and maybe it's true, what Dad sometimes says. You just keep living forward, for as long as you possibly can.

The Stories Are All Right Here

It smells like old newspapers at the train depot. There are crows by the tracks pecking for crumbs, a few pennies smashed on the rails, put there for luck, I guess, and left there.

I pick one up and slip it into the pouch with the map and Ilke's card, the special delivery and the pictures.

Two men in gray look-alike suits and a woman in dark jeans wait on the cracked platform not far from Hawk and me, staring down the tracks, wishing on the train, but they must have come from a few towns over because I don't know them, and they don't know me, and so far, our plan is working.

Luck.

So far Amber Green has sold us the tickets easy, no questions asked, just took our cash and handed us what we told her we needed and went straight back to watching her little TV, and now the train is actually coming. The shake of it starting in my feet and bringing a breeze with it, the winds of Chicago, which is where this train started its chug. Chicago to Lionsberg to Harrisburg to Philadelphia.

The 8:05 express.

All aboard.

We're in.

Plenty of seats. Plenty of people, too, who are fast asleep, their faces pressed against the scratched train glass, or their heads thrown back against the cushions, their crossword puzzles stuffed inside the train's seat pockets. Hawk and I find our place and slide in. I put the leather pouch between us. I press my hand against my heart, hold its pieces in place, its big swell of too muchness, and we're doing this, we're on the way. The conductor comes by for our tickets.

"Hawk," I say, when the conductor goes past, when it's just Hawk listening, when we're safely pulled away and nobody's come to stop us. "You sold your Scribners."

Hawk lifts one hand. Points to his head. "The stories are all right here," he says.

And what am I supposed to do but sit here and believe him.

The train rolls on. The world pulls past. The farms and the barns and the cows and the roads and the river out there, the churches and the houses and the cars driving parallel to the tracks, then just the land again, a rocky hill, another stretch of the river. Hawk puts his Spyglass up and reports on it, quiet, so the sleepers won't hear. I close my eyes. I listen. I see it the way Hawk calls it, the way I remember it from all the times in the pickup truck, heading from home to Philadelphia, to the elevators like refrigerators, to the doctors and their machines, their ruining numbers.

They call it an aortic rupture. They say that when it happens, you may feel yourself ripping in half. You feel it and you know that there isn't much time left, that even if you lived next door to the best hospital ever, the smartest surgeons on the planet, the greatest and most mighty machines, even if your health insurance was good enough, even if the banks said a big easy yes to everything you'd need, even if the banks believed you—the clock is ticking, and besides, there's a hardly-there percent of Marfan people who get out of that situation alive. There's too much blood now, in the wrong places. There's too much of everything wrong with you, and you should have fixed this when you could, before you broke.

Rich people would fix the bulge and they'd live on.

Rich people with good insurance, with money to spend on the extra things that that insurance will not pay for. Rich people, whose machines, and lives, do not go bust.

Nothing love can do to save you once the bulge gives out.

I know that.

I think about that.

I won't think about that anymore.

Not today.

Not tomorrow.

I'm done with worrying. For now.

We pull into Harrisburg and stop. More people get in, more men in mostly gray suits, women with phones up to their heads, briefcases hanging from straps, tickets in hands, more polystyrene tea, and still the people from Chicago sleep, the train smells like forest berries and sleep, the train pulls away from Harrisburg, keeps going.

Hawk keeps a lookout on.

I listen to him and his whisper reports.

I see it like he tells it.

I Could Be Anyone

Eleven fifteen. The glass faces of Philadelphia's towers are catching all the sky and sun. I watch over Hawk's shoulders and I see it—the diamond cuts of building tops, the old redbrick and the fresh white—until the bright outside goes dark as the train pulls into a tunnel. We stop. This is 30th Street Station, final stop. Everybody's standing and reaching and straightening, dumping their trash. Hawk and I wait, Hawk's Spyglass hanging loose around his neck and the soft pouch strapped to my shoulder.

Behind us, the kid who got on at Harrisburg, the only kid in this car, starts shouting in what he must think is a whisper. "Look," he's saying. "Look." He sees a giant, he says, a real live giant, right here on this train, does his mom see it? Look. He says it again, and his voice dials up. "Mom," he says. "Look. Do you see it?"

It.

I don't turn around, but I stare. I stare at that kid through the back of my head.

"The real BFG!" the kid calls out. "The actual one!" His mother shhhhs, but it's done: my face turns red, my heart bangs hard, I will not turn around. Hawk leans close and says, "Just a kid, Sara. Just a kid." I straighten the strap on my shoulder, breathe in and exhale, say nothing, not even to Hawk, and we stand there, caught in the crowd of passengers who have started turning their heads, looking for the giant that I am.

My hair's rainwater clean. I've got my best dress on, blue from the neck to the waist and green from the waist to the knees. I'm wearing my own best pair of flip-flops. Last night, when I couldn't sleep, after we'd grabbed the map, I stole downstairs again, Hawk's flashlight in my fist, and opened the door to the pantry. I shined the light on the shelf where Mom keeps what she calls her accessories, including the basket of paint for her toes. She calls the shelf Mom's Shelf, and we know, because she always says, that it is hers and only hers, don't touch, but I touched. I snagged a bottle of blue polish and a bottle of green and I followed the flashlight light back up the stairs and sat on the edge of my bed, painting my toenails, Mom-style. Maybe my arms are blushing now, my legs, my feet, but my toenails are not, and now the train doors open, and the passengers file forward, and we're out.

Out with the crowd, up the escalator into a station room so big and tall I could stand on my own shoulders a dozen times and still not touch the ceiling. We stand there, Hawk and me, looking in one direction, then in the other, trying to remember which set of far doors to the east or west leads to the buses that we always see on our way to the hospital of Dr. G.

The station signs read 29th Street on one side and 30th Street on the other. We decide on 30th Street, past the information booth and its sign, past the police dogs on their leashes, through the doors, and into the sun. The buses are here. There's a vendor selling hot dogs with steaming sauerkraut.

"Breakfast," Hawk says.

We buy ourselves some.

We join the New York City line, eating our hot dogs out of their paper trays, sharing a Coke to wash it all down.

Nobody's worried about us two kids out where we are, because we don't look like two kids, exactly. I pass for sixteen, seventeen, eighteen, maybe. I'm so tall I'm Hawk's much older sister, or maybe his young aunt, or maybe a family friend—doesn't matter. Out here, where people judge you for how you look, I am plenty old enough.

They open the luggage doors of the New York City bus and the passengers toss their suitcases in. They tell us boarding will start in just a few, and we're watching the crowd—the tattoos on the muscles of a girl near us, the cigarette smoke of a really old man, a toddler bouncing on a father's shoulders, a woman in a head scarf who stands perfectly still, a book cracked open in her hand. Hawk asks if I remember that part in *Treasure Island*.

"Which part?"

"'We were met and saluted, as we stepped aboard,'" Hawk recites.

"All aboard," the bus guy says.

They're reading the tickets, they're nodding people in. They're helping the lady with the cane, and now the little kid, and the woman with the tattoos takes a pink unicorn out of her bag and makes it talk until the kid stops howling.

We're next.

We find some seats, and there's no stopping us, there's no turning back.

Signs Ahead for Lincoln Tunnel

After we ramp up to the highway, it's all the same. Bunch of lanes going in our direction and bunch of lanes going in the other, and the cars and the cars and the trucks and the signs that Hawk and I start counting: Exit 7, Exit 7A, Exit 8, Exit 8A, all the way up the New Jersey Turnpike, which I have never seen, Hawk either.

The sky is blue, but most of the land's not green.

Hawk watches it go by, telling me some of what he sees, growing quieter and more quiet. I move the bag from my shoulder to my lap and snap it open. I arrange the loose parts of The Mister's *Roundabouts: Book Three*. The jewel eyes of a goat. The summer snow inside a barn. Two blue eggs on a torn truck seat. A tall shadow falling beneath the green of trees.

My shadow.

Like he's built each picture out of drops of rain.

Like I could ever understand, but I can't. Like I could ever know how he came to us and how Ilke found him. I slip the special delivery out of the pouch and read it again, stopping in between the words to study The Mister's drawings. Our lives through his eyes through his colors.

"What are you doing?" Hawk asks, his eyes finding my eyes through the reflection of the bus glass.

"Practicing," I say, "for Ilke."

He picks the drawings up and shuffles through one by one. He reads the special delivery.

"So she knows we're coming," Hawk says.

"Not really exactly," I say.

Hawk's brow wrinkles up. "I thought you said—"

"What I did was I asked the receptionist if Ilke would be in," I say.

"You're kidding, right? That's all you asked? I thought—" His cheeks have gone pink. His nose freckles scrunch.

"If Ilke is in, she'll have to see us, right? Can't not see us, if we've come this far. And besides, she promised you a reward. Who's to say that you're not there for the collecting?"

"All this," Hawk says, still not believing. "All this and we don't have an appointment? An actual appointment?" He slams his head back against the seat.

He snorts like Old Moe.

Rubs one eye with a fist.

Doesn't say anything else, turns to the window. I watch his face in the glass, the way he's watching the road, the way he's looking for something, always looking, and suddenly I remember the first time Hawk ever heard the word Marfan, and what he did about it.

Mom served out extra-wide slices of pie that night. She was trying to explain, to both of us, the word and what it meant. "'Marfan syndrome is caused by a defect (or mutation) in the gene that tells the body how to make fibrillin-1,'" she was reading, from a brochure the doctor had given her. "'This mutation results in an increase in a protein called transforming growth factor beta, or TGF-B. The increase in TGF-B causes problems in connective tissues throughout the body, which in turn create the features and medical problems associated with Marfan syndrome and some related disorders.'"

Mom looked up at us, to see if we were following. Dad was beside her, holding her hand. I could tell that she was trying hard, but even she couldn't understand the words that she had read off the brochure. That maybe Mom would never understand. That maybe it would always sound wrong and would never make sense, no matter how many times she read it.

"So basically," Hawk said, because nobody else was talking by then, because the pie was sitting there leaking its sweet strawberry juice, because no one was eating, not even Figgis, who had jumped onto the table. "Basically what you're saying is that Sara's sort-of-but-not-really one of a kind."

"Yeah," Mom said, putting the brochure down, looking at Hawk across the table, her eyes like his eyes, astronomical and liquid. "That's exactly what I'm saying."

We're at Exit 14.

Signs ahead for Lincoln Tunnel.

They Weren't Supposed to Know, They Know

New York City is not Philadelphia is not the farm. It's crowded and tight and shadowy, even now, two thirty in the afternoon. Hawk draws his fingers down the streets on the map. Calls out the instructions so I'll remember. Just past this. Just past that. Cross the street and walk and cross and at one point we will see it: The Flatiron Building, which looks like a slice of pie as tall as twenty-two stories.

There's no stopping because the crowds push on, because once we get onto one street, we're jostled toward another by people and briefcases and leashed dogs. When the lights turn red we stop to catch our breath, but when there's a gap in the buses and the taxis and the cars, the bikes, we're running.

Hawk always arriving to the opposite curb first.

Hawk waiting for me while the crowd rushes.

The sun falls in patches. The cars and the taxis honk like geese. We're onto Broadway now, which cuts an angle. We're still walking, and past the car lots and the shops and the towers, the buildings that look like all walls and no doors, and the restaurants that open out onto the walks. The birds are chubby here, white and gray. They peck around, sit on the signs, dig into the trash. Hawk stops to study the map again. Looks up to read street signs. Five blocks, he says, and we keep going, and there's so much pressure, and this better work.

Has to work.

We get a red light and we stop, all the force of the crowd against us. My hands on my pouch, Hawk's Spyglass at his neck, Hawk looking around, and now he grabs my hand and shouts.

"It's them!" he says. "They're here! Sara!"

I don't know what he's talking about. I can't see what he sees. The crowd is pressing and Hawk has stopped and now he yanks my arm and we're running again, and I'm not supposed to run, so we stop running. We just walk. We walk. We weave. Hawk ahead, me yelling, "Who?"

"Them," he says, calling the words out, over his shoulder. "Mom and Dad with The Mister driving. And Mrs. Kalin in the backseat."

"Can't be!" I yell, but of course it can be, of course I know that our leaving was no secret—that Isaiah knew and Mrs. Kalin knew and Amber Green knew, and when there are only a handful of people in the place where you live, word gets out fast, if your mom starts making calls, and so I guess she had to be making calls, and I know one clue could be connected to another and that by the time my mom got to Mrs. Kalin, it had to be clear as day where half the Scholls had gone.

I turn my head to see what I can see.

Hawk turns and hurries me.

"I thought that whale was stuck," I say, walking faster and faster.

"Dad must have dug it out."

"I thought—"

"Driving's faster than a train and a wait and a bus," Hawk says. "But now they're in a car and we're on a sidewalk, and they are stuck in traffic, and we are not, so hurry, Sara, hurry. We're doing what we came to do."

"I can't go any faster," I say.

"You are going to go faster," Hawk says, taking the pouch from me, taking anything he can to make this easier, and now he's holding my hand, and he's walking my speed, and we hug the shadows where we can. We zag through the crowds. The taxis and the cars and the buses honk. Across 25th. Across 24th. The triangle of the Flatiron is not far from here, not far.

The Flatiron is here.

Hawk holds the door.

We're in.

However and Notwithstanding

"We have a meeting with Ilke Vanderveer," Hawk says to the lobby man.

The man looks up from his narrow stone desk and his flat computer screen. He squints.

"Three o'clock," Hawk says, taking little sips of air at a time. "We're a smidgeon early."

I'm way out of breath, now smoothing my hair, now taking my pouch back and moving it from one shoulder to the other, wondering how Hawk knows how to talk like this. Which Scribner did he read this in? Which quote is he borrowing? The lobby man gives us a funny look. He picks up his phone. He asks who he might say is asking.

"Hawk Scholl," Hawk says, then leans up, like he's conspiring with the guy. "It's about the reward."

"The reward," the lobby man repeats, turning his face to one angle, lifting his chin. "I'll be sure to mention the reward."

The phone rings through. The man waits. I look around at the lobby. The arch overhead. The stone on the walls. The lonely American flag drooping off its brass stand. There's a bank of elevators held between marble walls. That's where we want to be. We're waiting.

"That's right," the man is saying now into the phone. "Boy and a young woman. Claiming a three o'clock and a reward.

"Yes," he says. "I'll wait."

So he waits.

So we wait.

So Hawk paces and I watch the street for taxis, cars, and one long Silver Whale.

"Uh-huh," the lobby man says now.

"That's what she says?" he says, listening.

"Roger that. Not a problem. I'll relay the message.

"Ilke Vanderveer is in a meeting," he says now, hanging up.

Hawk stops in his back-and-forth tracks. I feel my hopes fall. I think of everything we've done and the trouble we're in and the promise I made to Hawk that we could do this, that Ilke would see us, that we would—

"However and notwithstanding," the lobby man continues now, "Ms. Vanderveer's assistant asks that you come on up. You'll be seen when the meeting is done."

Hawk shoots up so straight he's just a head shorter than me. He polishes the Spyglass around his neck with a touch of his finger.

"Sir," he says, on his way to the elevator banks.

"Sara," he calls.

I'm coming.

Do Your Best

It's not as glamorous up here on the sixth floor of the Flatiron as it is in the lobby down below. Cardboard boxes in the narrow hallways and stains on the nubby gray carpet and places on the wall where posters must have been, because the paint is different shades of olive. Shelves and shelves and shelves of books, the covers facing out, gold stars pasted on their covers. There's a vase of new flowers on the reception desk. There's a big clock with golden hands ticking out the hour.

Past a crush of desks behind half-there walls, there's a room with a smudgy door. A skinny girl who doesn't look much older than me and is maybe half as tall leads us through the maze, past the olive walls, and opens the door, her big beautiful curly hair arranged around her head like a halo. She asks if we'd like water.

"Please," Hawk says.

"Make that two," I say. I'm desperate thirsty. Hungry, too. Feels like a whole other year ago when we were eating hot dogs and kraut.

The girl leaves. She comes back. She puts two glasses on the round table, the two charms on her long necklace ringing.

We can see the streets from the room's one window, the traffic still in a craze, and that's where we stand, by the window. Hawk twists toward 23rd Street to see what he can see. "No whale in sight," he says.

Like that will last. It won't. I hear that golden-handed clock out there ticking. Who knows how long Ilke will keep us waiting, how long before we're found out, here, by Mom and Dad, by The Mister, by Mrs. Kalin.

I am sorry, very sorry, I can already hear myself.

I am sorry, but I had to.

I am sorry, please don't be mad.

I am sorry, but please, just listen.

I try to imagine that Silver Whale swimming off the farm, Dad shoving his weight into it, Mom, too. I try to imagine The Mister in the front seat, revving the engine—his cycle, his suitcase, his drawings, his stuff, some of his drawings missing. I try to imagine their whole drive here, and before that: Mom looking for me in the barn with the goats. Dad looking for Hawk by the pigs. Mom finding my note and running outside to find Dad, past the cats, past Phooey and the peahens, past Figgis.

The Mister came to us for peace.

And now look at what has happened.

Hawk and I stand at the window, just looking down, just waiting. We stand here and the world can splinter in two for all the tension we are feeling.

The doorknob rattles. The door opens wide. Ilke Vanderveer is here. In a pale pink dress with pale pink shoes whose toes look sharp as weapons. She's got her eyelashes on and her eyes look heavy.

"Hawk Scholl," she says, her lips sticking to her teeth when she talks.

"Ms. Vanderveer," he answers. Like a pro.

"I understand that you have news for me."

"Indeed," Hawk says. "We do. This is Sara."

"I thought I said—"

"Brother," Hawk says, pointing to himself. "Sister. We keep no secrets from each other."

I extend my arm to shake Ilke's hand. She gives me a quick grip and a long up and down, stopping at my polka-dotted toenails. She pulls out a chair.

"Please," she says. Suggesting we join her.

Hawk and I each take our seats.

I get my pouch prepared.

Ilke raps her pink nails on the table.

"What did Martin say," she asks now, "when you gave him the package?"

"Well," Hawk says.

"As you recall," Ilke says, after Hawk does not continue, "the only reward here is for a job completed. Proof of my letter, delivered. A verifiable response."

"We are in possession of your letter," I say, pulling out her own special delivery and trying to sound like Hawk.

Her heavy eyes open as much as they can, which isn't very much.

"We also have this," I say, pulling out the sketch of Jolly's face. "And this." Digging in for the other pictures I stole, but really more like borrowed.

"Do you have a copy of *Roundabouts: Book Two?*" Hawk says, leaning toward Ilke, over the table.

Ilke sits there, not answering. There's a sleek white phone on the table. She thinks for a while, then punches the 0. Tells the person on the other end to bring her Two this very minute.

The skinny girl opens the door. Delivers the book. Leaves us.

"So," Hawk says. "As you can see," he says, opening the book, thumbing through pages, starting this, all business-ish, like he hasn't spent his whole life on a farm, fixing tractors and watering pigs and climbing the limbs of the *Hispaniola*. Like we have all the time in the world, here, on the sixth floor of the Flatiron, the Silver Whale floating through Manhattan.

"As you can see, we have here, at the end of *Book Two*, a pair of red shoes perched on a cliff. Behind the shoes is where the shoes have been. All the beautiful red shoe places."

"I'm familiar with the book," Ilke says, her lips sticking.

"Now, on the other side of the cliff," Hawk continues, "is a stretch of farm, a humble working place, with humble people. You can see it here." He points. "Tiny dots. Tiny, but it's clear."

Ilke's eyes dart back over to the special delivery, exposed on the table as Hawk talks. They flicker back to try to get a better view of what we've brought with us.

"Very familiar," she repeats.

"Turns out The Mister has a plan for *Book Three*," Hawk continues. "Turns out he's taking his red shoes to this old run-down farm, where there are cows and pigs and shadows. Turns out he wants his red shoes to live. He does not want his red shoes to vanish."

I lay the sketches out now, one beside the other, the sketches turned to face Ilke so that she can better see them. She leans in, lowers her head. She reaches for them. Gently. Holds them up to the light. Holds them closer to her eyes. Then puts them down and folds one hand into the other.

"Well, that's some trick," she says. We can barely hear her.

"No trick at all," Hawk says.

"What kind of game does he think we're playing? Sending you back here with these. These sketches and my note. A confidential note. Special delivery."

"The Mister's not playing any game," Hawk says, sitting even straighter.

"I beg to differ," Ilke answers. She pushes back into her chair. She crosses her arms.

"He didn't send us here," I say. "He doesn't know we're here. I mean, he wasn't supposed to know. We didn't tell him. He never read your letter."

"I beg your pardon?" She crosses her arms even tighter.

"We read it," I say. "We read your letter."

She pushes back her chair to stand.

"There are laws—" she starts.

"I took the sketches out of the back of his car," I talk over her. I talk over her, but nicely.

"You *took* them." Ilke narrows her eyes and I can see us as she sees us—two kid thieves from a pig and chicken farm way out in the middle of Mountain Dale nowhere.

"There were plenty more. A whole book's worth. Except that some of them aren't finished."

"Is that a fact?"

"We tell the truth," Hawk says.

Most of the time, I think. *In regular circumstances.*

Ilke uncrosses her arms. She puts her elbows on the table. She fits her chin into her palms. She studies us and I can see how her eyes are small beneath her lids, her eyes are coal bits, burning. "Why have you come?" she says. "There's no reward in this. Surely you must know that. Surely you must see that I'm a very busy woman. Surely it must occur to you—"

"We came because The Mister has packed to leave and he can't leave," I say, my words real fast, my heart real urgent. "We came because he has to finish *Book Three* the way he wants to finish *Book Three*. We came because he doesn't want those shoes to vanish. Because he wants to write his own ending, and in his ending, the shoes keep walking. We can see them walking."

"We came"—Hawk clears his throat—"on his behalf."

"We came," I say, "because we like him." And we do, I think, we really do. We like his imagination.

"You have no right," Ilke says, her cheeks red, her voice gravel. "To interfere. This is none of your business. The audacity of it. The nerve! You"—she looks for a word, she tries to find it—"interlopers!"

She squints.

She stares.

I am not afraid.

"You came to us," I say.

"You gave me the letter," Hawk says.

"I gave you instructions," she says, "and you—"

"We're two of M. B. Banks's half a million readers," Hawk says calmly. "We're focus group material. We're statistics." I look at him. I smile at him. I will never, in my life, however long it is, forget this.

"We believe in the shoes," I say. "We've come to tell you that in person."

"Because you're in charge," Hawk says.

"Because you can change things," I say, leaning across the table now, sliding the pictures back toward her, laying them out, the start or the middle or the end of his story.

The look in Ilke's eyes is something between ashamed and furious. She sputters out the start of words but doesn't finish them. Now she pushes back and stands and crosses the room. She fixes herself at the window, looking down into the street.

"Do you know what it is," she says, "to walk around each day with my responsibilities? To satisfy our readers? We need big hits. Bestsellers. Revenues bigger than advances. Do you know what that's like?"

"No," Hawk admits. "We don't."

"Do you know how the trends insist? How we need to tell the stories we think the readers want to read? We do our math on this. We watch our Ps, we watch our *Ls*. Profits," she explains now. "And losses."

"But what's the matter with The Mister's story?" I ask. "What's the matter with the red shoes finding their way back home to this farm after they've been all around the world?"

I say it, and when I say it, I suddenly know. I say it and I look at Hawk and his eyes are big because he knows it too.

The Mister's red shoes are coming home.

Our farm is The Mister's home.

Or his idea of home.

Or it could be.

He's drawn his red shoes home.

"He's got a contract," Ilke says. "A contract is a promise. He's already a full year late with his story."

"Not every promise can be kept," I say. I think of my seeds in the museum by that wall. Some will sprout and some will not. Some will yield and some won't.

Ilke touches her forehead to the window glass, and she's thinner, I realize, than I thought she was. She's thin, and she could break. Like any one of us.

"We've come to ask you to give his story a chance," I say. "We come because we hope you will. But now we should be going."

I stand and Hawk does. I pack up my pouch. Mom and Dad will be here soon.

We'll have a ton of explaining to do.

We Need a Better Explanation

They're rushing through the lobby entry when we're trying to rush out. Mom and Dad, and The Mister, and Mrs. Kalin. Mom's face has every picture in it, every drop of color and every kind of line. Dad is rubbing his head. Mrs. Kalin is in her flowered dress, and The Mister—he's standing there without his stick. He's looking at us, he's looking around, he's looking: snow on snow on snow, his blue vest and his red shoes on.

He calls the lobby man by his first name, Tony.

He catches my eye, smiles. Maybe he nods a little bit. Maybe he touches his hands together, those long fingers. Maybe he says thank you. Maybe I hear him.

"Sweetie," Mom keeps saying. "Sweetie." Her name for Hawk and me, for both of us, the only name she has right now.

"We thought—" Dad says.

"You should have—" Dad tries to start again, but it doesn't matter, because nobody needs words right now. Sometimes life is just about the pictures.

"Martin."

I hear Ilke's voice and I turn. I see her standing there, in that stone lobby, on her wobbling shoes. "Martin, may I talk to you?" she says, and I know she's trying for her in-charge voice, but it doesn't sound in charge at all.

It sounds more like a question.

The Mister walks toward her, leaving us behind. They disappear around the corner, toward the alcove where the elevators are. I can't hear what they're saying because Hawk is trying to explain—about the train, about the bus, about the things that we discovered. Hawk is the only one who's talking.

"We had to," Hawk is saying. "We didn't have a choice." He stands near Mom and Dad, looking up, pleading with his moon eyes, his pale face, his summer freckles. He'll talk for us. I'll let him.

Mom's got her hand on Hawk's shoulder. Dad's got his hand around Mom's waist. Mrs. Kalin is smoothing the flowers on her skirt, and I look at her. She smiles.

"I understand." I hear Ilke's voice now. "Yes. Yes. Your prerogative." I hear The Mister's voice, from around the same corner. It's softer than hers is, but it sounds like *thank you*, and now I hear Ilke say, in a different tone, that she always loved those shoes, that she'll always be proud of editing *Book One* and *Book Two*.

And right this moment, nobody else is talking. Right this moment we're all trying to hear, to be sure, and when The Mister appears, we see his red shoes first. And then we see him smiling.

Inside the Silver Whale

Inside the Silver Whale it bumps and rattles.

Inside the Silver Whale it smells like color.

Inside the Silver Whale the one wheel of the unicycle spins and goes nowhere, and Mom and Dad sit with The Mister up front, and Hawk and I sit with each other in the back with the brushes and the box, the pictures that were drawn, the pictures that were not. We sit with the suitcase, and we sit with the other stuff that we can't explain, and Mrs. Kalin isn't here beside us because she had some New York City places she said she hoped to go.

"There's a big library up on Fifth Avenue," she said,

with stars in her eyes. "I always wanted to see it."

"You kids," Mom says, and keeps turning around, like she's seeing us for the very first time, or like we've been gone for a year or maybe three. She says she'll get mad soon enough but right now she's mostly grateful. "All the way grateful," she corrects herself, and Dad drives and now The Mister shakes his head.

"George would have loved this," he says, and we ask to know who George is and he waits and he watches the road and he says, "Your father already knows; we talked about it on the way up."

"Dad?" we say.

"Dad?"

But now Dad is wiping a tear from his face and he can't talk, so The Mister does. Hawk and I scrunch up as close as the whale's seat belts will let us.

This Is Not How the Story Ends

Turns out George was The Mister's best friend, back in another century, when The Mister was a kid. Turns out George was Howard George Scholl, who was my dad's own dad. Turns out Howard George was my granddad and that when he was a kid, for one month every summer, The Mister came to Mountain Dale, the prettiest land around. He came to Mountain Dale because George was here, and because they were best friends, thanks to their parents.

Turns out that you have no idea how any story's going to end.

Turns out that some stories end right at the start, which means they make a circle.

Turns out that I'm glad for how well I hear. I don't need a Spyglass for this story.

The Mister played in the shed on the hill when he was a kid, he told us in his Silver Whale, while Dad drove and Mom kept her hand on his wrist. The Mister climbed in our tree (he says it was much smaller then). The Mister fed the pigs, which didn't have *Treasure Island* names. The Mister milked the goats, but they had horns. The Mister ate the tomatoes that grew here and the jam my great-grandmother made. The Mister knows how some of the things that are still broken got broken, and he says someday he'll tell us.

The Mister was here every summer as a kid. George never left the farm. The Mister went off, around the world, moved from place to place as an artist. The Mister was far away, in a town called Verona, when the accident that killed my grandparents occurred. Two people that I never met and Mom only knew long enough to learn a little pie and Dad never talked about, because maybe it hurt too much for him to say what happened to them, or maybe we never asked my dad the right questions, or maybe when you're the kid you think the biggest stories are your own.

"I never forgave myself for all the time I spent away," The Mister said, after his long story was coming to an end. "I never forgave myself, and I always wanted to come back, and then I saw your 'For Rent' ad, and I knew where I was going."

"Best story," Hawk said. "Ever."

"I wanted to tell you," The Mister said. "I wanted to, but I didn't know how. I never was so good with words. I was always much better with pictures."

Dad drove silent, after The Mister's story was done. He drove down the hills and up the hills and then to Mountain Dale. He drove us under the skirt shade of the trees and past the pigs and toward Figgis and Scaredy and Old Moe and the peacocks and also Phooey, who had started to worry that we'd all gone free range.

There's stale sourdough left over, there's Jane's jam. There's Mildred's best and our fresh eggs and Isaiah's square of cheese. Whatever we have, it's for all of us, The Mister here included. Whatever there is, there is. Mom says she'd have made a pie if she'd known what was to come, and then Mom says that's it better, isn't it, when the surprise is the surprise you weren't expecting.

We've turned the lights off overhead and lit the candles. We've let the cats in the house, and they're behaved. When Old Moe makes his warthog sounds in the barn outside beside the hay shed that is no more hay shed, Dad does not apologize. He shrugs, the good kind of sad smile on his face.

"I remember," The Mister has been saying, he keeps saying. "I remember." And he remembers almost everything. He remembers it with words. The smell of the farm air. The whisper of the candle. The nonsense of the goats and hens and pigs. The Mister remembers and he takes us all back to the farm we love and the life we're grateful for every day that ends, every day that starts.

The Mister says the pond was always where it is, but it was deeper. He says the hills were always the hills, but they seemed steeper. He says he used to climb the trees and look far out and imagine himself as anything in every place—small and big and far and near, with plenty more to imagine.

"*Roundabouts: Book Three* will be my last book," he says. "My own book, published or maybe not. *Book Three* will be the end, but not really. The journey never stops."

"Lucky," Mom says, shaking her head, finding a curl of hair, making it curl harder on her finger. "Lucky we posted the ad."

"Lucky you helped," Dad says, nodding to the rest of us, "build the lighthouse." Meaning Hawk. Meaning me. Meaning us, the Scholls.

Mom tucks her hair back into her bandanna. Her eyes catch the light from the candle flame.

I look at Hawk. He looks at me. He claps his hands

over his mouth to keep his feelings in, but I'm letting my feelings out—I'm letting all the things built up inside of me be all the things I am. I'm crying like the best worst rain.

"Your mom and dad have been talking to me, Sara," The Mister says now. "Your mom and dad have told me stories."

I don't know what he means. I know what he means. I wait.

"I'd like to do what I can to help," The Mister says. "I'd like to get you that operation, if you let me. Giving to you would be me giving straight back to George, and I never thought there'd be a way, but maybe you're the way. Maybe you can help me, Sara. Say yes, and I'll be happy."

I feel my breath go quick. I feel my eyes go hot. I look at Hawk and we are silent silent silent and then he raises his fist. I raise my fist back. We go knuckle to knuckle. The smallest, gentlest, swiftest tap, and now Phooey makes the loudest noise when we begin to laugh.

Acknowledgments

Becca Weust came into my life in the early months of 2016, when I began to write her story on behalf of Accolade, a corporate client for whom I write stories about patient care and health access. Steam was rising from a mug of forest-berry tea as we talked. There were fantasy novels and college texts on the Greco-Roman world on the shelf near her bed, a tuxedo cat named Figgis on the prowl among her bedsheets, and a big computer screen nearby, where sometimes Becca played e-sports and sometimes, instead, researched the connective tissue disorder Marfan syndrome, with which she had been diagnosed as a child. Becca had faced many complications from the syndrome—heart surgery and brutalizing headaches; a collapsing sternum and the deepest exhaustion; long, long stretches spent in bed, which is to say, not at school and not out with friends, and not down the street at a café, and now, not at the job she would be so good at doing.

Those with Marfan tend to be taller, longer, thinner, more curved than those without it. They also face the risk of the enlargement or tear of the aorta, the large artery that takes blood away from the heart; sudden lung collapse; severe vision issues; and early death. Surgeries can be complicated and expensive. Lives can be severely compromised. Some two hundred thousand individuals in the US have Marfan or a related condition, but experts say that perhaps half are undiagnosed. Many people are altogether unaware of this condition.

In the years since our first telephone conversation, Becca has emailed photographs of Figgis and blooming lavender and the purple-icing cake she managed to make during a spell of being better for a while. She has signed her notes "Amor Vincit Omnia" and "Yours with all the Himalayan rock salt your ions can handle" and "love" and "PS: Yesterday is a day for Aortic Aneurysm Awareness."

She has educated me.

"For a while it felt like too many things were broken without any kind of resource to fix them," she once wrote. "It was really difficult coming to terms with the idea that even if there is a 'fix' for this, I will very likely be reliant on others much more than I will ever be comfortable with. Finding a way to trade a dream of independence and self-reliance for something else, a something that I'm still struggling to feel a worthiness or balance in. People like to say that laughter is the best medicine, but I like to say salt is the best preservative."

Becca has helped me understand what it is to live honestly and gracefully with uncertainty and pain, and when I asked if I might write a story not *about* her, but *for* her, she said yes. Sara, my main character, is not, then, Becca; Sara does not face nearly the number of challenges that life has brought Becca's way. But Sara has a cat named Figgis and she's extremely smart about seeds, and she knows a thing or two about baking, and most of all, she's brilliant and funny and determined and questing and curious and real, and there would be no Sara without Becca.

Marfan syndrome lies at the heart of this novel, but Marfan hardly defines my twelve-year-old Sara Scholl. Sara lives her life on a farm in rural Pennsylvania with a *Treasure Island*–obsessed brother named Hawk, a character whose kindness and grit and literary insights are inspired by a former student and now most-excellent teacher, David Marchino. The farm itself was inspired by Mountain Dale Farm, an idyllic Civil War–era expanse nestled against a hill in central Pennsylvania. It was here, at Mountain Dale, that my husband and I met with our first group of Juncture Workshop writers—Annie, Hannah, Jessica, Karen, Kirsten, Lynn, Starr, Tam, Toby, Tracey, Wendy—to learn the language of ourselves and that land, to count the peacocks and scatter the chickens, to wait for the rain to fall. I am eternally grateful to Sally and Ken and their family—generous hosts in a historic place. Sally read this book with utmost care. I am grateful to her for that too.

For their willingness to review the text for any errors I might have made regarding Marfan syndrome, I am extremely grateful to Eileen Masciale, the chief program officer of The Marfan Foundation, and Josephine Grima, PhD, the Foundation's chief science officer. The Marfan Foundation was founded in 1981, at a time when little was known about Marfan and related disorders. It was established to "advance research, serve as a resource for families and health care providers, and raise public awareness," and when my note came in asking for help, it was answered, kindly, at once. Any residual errors are mine alone.

For being Becca's strong advocate through many years of her health care odyssey, and for talking to me by phone after doing extra research on my behalf, I am unspeakably grateful to Amy Schmidheiser of Accolade, whose goodness is a permeating force. For cofounding Accolade and inviting me into its world, for all the conversations we have had about what matters to us and what might matter to the world, I thank my cherished friend, Accolade co-founder, Tom Spann.

Caitlyn Dlouhy was supremely instrumental in helping me reimagine this story and find its right ending. Karen Grencik brought her big heart to all the years when these pages were underway. Levente Szabó produced a stunningly perfect cover within the frame of a jacket designed by Debra Sfetsios-Conover. Valerie Shea and Jeannie Ng were gentle and thorough and appreciated. N. C. Wyeth's masterful illustrations of *Treasure Island* and other Scribner Classics hang at the Brandywine River Museum of Art, where I've spent many days thinking about, and sharing, Hawk's literary obsession. Debbie Levy and Ruta Septys bolstered me through long and treasured conversations. A young man named Oliver taught me indelible lessons about how to live. Alyson Hagy encourages me with her grace and intelligence. Mrs. Kalin, my second-grade teacher, was the first to believe in my own stories. My father helped me undertake research for the fire. My husband, Bill, listened and loved and lived that farm with me. Our son, Jeremy, remains the reason I search for, and try to, write (though it can take a long time, though there are many drafts) stories that can make a difference to those who find their way to them.

READING GROUP GUIDE FOR
The Great Upending

In *The Great Upending*, Sara Scholl and her brother, Hawk, live with their parents on a family farm among pigs and goats and fabulous chickens, vegetables, and housecats. It's a happy family, a beautiful place, but there are problems. A drought has set in; money is short; and Sara, who has Marfan syndrome, has been told that her future could depend on her getting medical care that her family cannot afford. Into this world moves an old man, a picture-book creator the children call The Mister, who is renting the family's renovated silo. The Mister has mysterious troubles all his own, and the children are cautioned against getting involved. Soon, the challenges all the characters face merge into a single, life-changing adventure.

Below are some questions you might consider now that you've read the book.

1. Sometimes, when Sara and Hawk sit outside, they listen to the sounds of their world: "The farm noises up. There are cows in the cow barn, goats in the goat barn, cats in their cuddle, and the old horse Moe, who snorts like a warthog." What are the sounds of your world? Make a list and then write a poem so that others can hear what you hear.

2. Hawk loves the book *Treasure Island* so much that he carries parts of it around with him in his head. Name the book that you love best, then write a letter to the author (even if the author is no longer alive) to tell them why.

3. Sara has her own private seed museum. What do the seeds mean to Sara? What is your hobby? Find a way to document that hobby with just four photographs.

4. Sara's mom can do a lot of things—fix a fence, fight a fire, bake delicious pies. In

fact, every member of the Scholl family has special talents. What are they? What do they contribute to the story?

5. Mrs. Kalin, who was inspired by Beth's second-grade teacher, is a very special librarian. In what ways does she make the books she loves come to life? Draw your version of the World's Best Library—and the world's best librarian.

6. When you first meet The Mister, what do you believe his story is? How does your impression of him change as the story unfolds?

7. Sara and Hawk have been asked, very clearly, not to interfere with The Mister. Why? Do you think they were wrong to get involved with him? Should they have told their parents what they were up to? How did this choice impact the outcome of the story?

8. The Mister is the creator of famous wordless picture books. Create your own wordless picture book and share it with people you love. Ask others to tell you the story they believe your wordless picture book tells. In what ways

are the stories your pictures inspire similar to the story you intended? In what ways are they different? What is the power of a story without words?

9. What do you think the red shoes in The Mister's picture book symbolize?

10. Marfan syndrome is a connective tissue disorder that has affected many famous people. Research the condition to find out more about its symptoms and the studies now being undertaken to help those who are diagnosed with it.

11. The author, Beth Kephart, dedicated this book to a young friend named Becca Weust, who has Marfan syndrome. To whom would you dedicate a poem or story of your own? Write and illustrate that poem or story, and include a dedication.

This guide has been provided by Simon & Schuster for classroom, library, and reading group use. It may be reproduced in its entirety or excerpted for these purposes.

Turn the page
for a sneak peek at

WILD BLUES

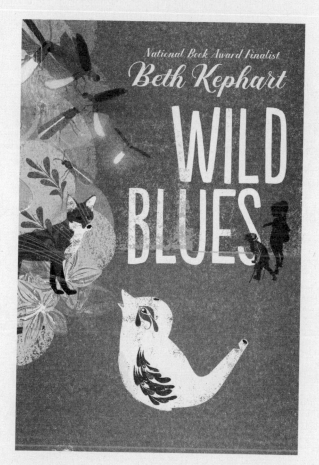

NOBODY IS JUST THEIR GENES, OR JUST THEIR proteins.

Nobody is only DNA.

I, for example, am Lizzie, pure Lizzie, and my uncle was my uncle and not the gossip people told, and my mother was my mom and not her cancer. We were all the all of who we were, and I'm going to tell my story straight through, and then, maybe then, you will tell yours. You will see how much it hurts to say the whole truth of who you are, plus the truth of all that happened.

This is a victim impact statement. Offered right here, from this bed, in this room, in this house, to you, because as you can see, I am not moving.

Another thing for this record, up front: Matias is a part of this story, and Matias was not his condition. So he had a problem with his pituitary gland. So it had turned his growth hormone off. So the only way

Matias had a chance of getting taller was by keeping to a schedule—an every-day shot of growth juice. All true. He'd had this done to him since he was small. He'd done it to himself since he was eight. Had gotten up each day and punched the needle in, but he was still so short, and he was running out of time. Matias wished for his shoes to grow small or his pants to grow short, but neither happened. He wished for a body that could run as fast as other bodies run.

He did not have a body that could run like that.

That body, that gland, is not who Matias was.

But some of that is part of this story.

You know a little. You were there. You played a part. You had firsthand news about the prison break down the road—the two men who popped up from a sewer hole with their hair combed back and their hello hands waving. The two men who were Hollywood inside their own heads, who were coming close to famous, who'd waited winter to spring to summer and now were on the move, and weren't just their DNA either, their genes.

Those two men had a choice.

They had an accomplice.

People ask me, was I afraid?

Not yet.

Not then.

But soon.

LET'S START IN SUNSHINE. LET'S START WITH the absolute true: My uncle was wild beauty in motion, and I was the one who knew. You couldn't trench a fence around him. Couldn't box him with a frame. He was in and out, there and here, a blaze of Day-Glo glory.

He loved me best. He told me so. I was his primo family. Which is why when Mom said, month before last, "Choose your summer adventure"—*choose*—I chose my uncle and his reno'ed schoolhouse cabin, his swatch of God's elastic earth, his way of laughing, which made me laugh, which made us both laugh harder. Anytime I got a choice, I always chose my uncle. I chose four highway hours north from here, one quick bump east, one cut up a diagonal road that quickly skinnied. I chose where the hills are almost mountains, and the trees are so green that the shade is black, and the loose gravel rattles the belly of the car.

And there are streams, and not just streams but something they call kettles.

I chose my uncle, which means I also chose my friend Matias. The three of us as indivisibles, or that's what I thought then.

Mom's hands were tight on the steering wheel. Her long black hair with its bright-white roots whipped around her head, tornado style.

"You ready?" she said.

I had my solo suitcase in the rear and my caterpillar backpack by my feet. I was wearing my turquoise Keens loose and my khaki shorts long to my knees. The bill of my Phillies cap was pointing back. I'd written emergency facts in the palms of both hands, and the ink was already sweating.

"Ready for anything," I said.

Don't miss any of these amazing novels from the winner of the National Book Award and the Newbery Medal, CYNTHIA KADOHATA:

SYLVIE & JULES, JULES & SYLVIE.
BEST FRIENDS, SISTERS.

Sylvie always wished one thing:

To run faster.
Faster than a deer.
Faster than a comet.

But when she vanishes one morning,
Jules only has one wish:

COME BACK.

MAYBE A FOX

KATHI APPELT AND ALISON McGHEE

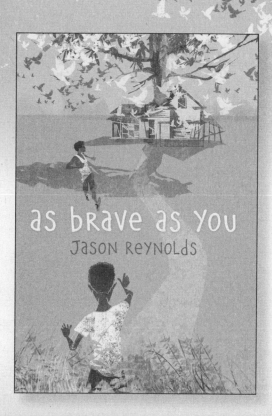

what does it mean to be brave?

At the beginning of summer, Genie thinks it's not being
afraid of Grandpop's dumb ol' dog.

Or trying to fix something important that he's broken.

But is that it? Or is it just as important to own up to
what you've done? Even if it's really, *really* bad?

EMA LIVES SOMEWHERE AMONG:
TWO COUNTRIES, TWO LANGUAGES, AND TWO TIME ZONES.

Then, when
tragedy strikes,
it seems like
the whole world
is living
somewhere
among: chaos,
fear, and
loneliness.

But among it all
remains
one thing:
HOPE.

FROM atheneum CAITLYN DLOUHY BOOKS
PRINT AND EBOOK EDITIONS AVAILABLE
simonandschuster.com/kids